IN PRAISE OF ISLAND WOMEN
& OTHER CRIMES

ALSO BY BRENDA FLANAGAN

You Alone are Dancing
Allah in the Islands

ACKNOWLEDGEMENTS

"The Water Woman" (published as "Small Island Pride") first appeared in the *Journal of Caribbean Studies*, Vol. 1, 1980; "On a Point of Order", in *Witness*, Vol. 1, Summer 1987; "The Green Card" in *Indiana Review*, Vol. 12, Winter 1988; "To Die of Old Age in a Foreign Country" in *Caliban*, Vol. 8, 1990, and in *African American Literature Anthology*, Ed. Al Young, New York, HarperCollins, 1996; "Gloria's Shop" in *Drumvoices*, Vol. 3, Winter, 1993-1994; "The Girl from Bahia" in *Caliban*, Fall 1994; "Habana Libre", in *Blossoming Trends*, 1994; "Homeless in O'ahu", in *Caliban*, Vol. 15, 1995; "Behind God's Back" in *Controlled Burn*, Vol. I, Winter, 1995; "The Stone Grower" in *Controlled Burn*, Vol. V, Winter 1999; "Sea Baths" in *Controlled Burn*, Vol. IX, Winter 2003.

BRENDA FLANAGAN

IN PRAISE OF ISLAND WOMEN
& OTHER CRIMES

SHORT FICTION

PEEPAL TREE

First published in 2005
by KaRu Press, USA
This revised and expanded edition is published in 2010
by Peepal Tree Press Ltd
17 King's Avenue
Leeds LS6 1QS
England

ISBN13: 9781845231279

This is a work of fiction. Any resemblance to real persons or
situations is not to be taken literally, but some people may do
so anyway, alas.

Supported by
ARTS COUNCIL
ENGLAND

Stories are never true. That's why we believe them.

For "Island" women everywhere.

CONTENTS

MY JOURNEY NOW START

And yet, it begin a long long time ago when Madam Grosdent's blood fell in the Diego Martin Valley where I was born, and I, like this she-man, this soucouyant, wake up black and blue, and I tell Echu to make me wide as the earth, and tall as the clouds, fast and clear as the rushing wind, and as strong as the mighty Caribbean sea, with a voice as loud as thunder, teeth large enough to bite rock, and a heart that will not break when it get hurt. He turned me into a ball of fire so I could light the footsteps of she-men as they grip Haitian hillsides with bare toes, trying to fashion a life out of the stones they inherit. And he make me a bee that sings sweet sweet like mango Julie of the jamettes and marabuntas, the marchands, and all they mauvais-langue women whose voices didn't sing so sweet before. And days when I get tired, he send me to the sea to dance in the salt water with Erzulie, so she could wash the blight from me, and I could come out fresh like a hibiscus opening up in the morning, and know, my journey now start.

SEA BATHS

My father comes on Sundays to take us for a sea bath. He does this once a month, the day after he pays Mr. Ling for the goods he allows my mother to trust from the shop. These two things my father does religiously: he takes me, my last sister and my youngest brother for a sea bath once a month, and he pays for the food my mother takes from the shop.

He says we need the sea baths to wash the blight away from us. He always says, *the blight*, as if it is a disease he knows that we carry, like chiggers in our toes in the dry season. Sometimes, when he says this, I think he means we might turn out like my brother whose words sput, sput, sputter like Mr. Ramotar's car in the rainy season. My father hates to hear my brother sputter and sometimes taps him on his head to make him hurry up the words, or he'll turn away before my brother finishes his sentence.

My father says it's my mother's fault that my brother can hardly speak but I am afraid to ask him how come. Children do not put their mouths in grown people's business. I wish I could find out where blight comes from but I don't know who to ask. I looked up the word in the dictionary in school but the explanation only confused me. It said: "*blight, v.t. To affect with blight; to cause to wither or decay; to frustrate-v.i. To injure as blight does.*" On another page "blight" was a noun but its origin was unknown. It was defined as "*Some influence, usually hidden or not conspicuous that destroys plants, arrests their growth, etc.; smut, mildew or other fungous plant disease; any insects which infects or destroys plants; any malignant influence of obscure or mysterious origin; anything which withers hope, blasts prospects, or checks prosperity.*"

When I see stains on clothes, like cashew juice or coconut water on my white school bodice, I always think of blight.

Nothing in this world will get out cashew juice and coconut stains. My mother tries the best she can. She scrubs my bodice against the ridges on the jucking board until her fingers turn blue, but the stains don't move. They run down the front of my clothes like the streaks on the diapers my mother wears on the days she bleeds. No matter how hard she washes those cloths, bleaching them on stones in the yard, leaving them outside in the dew overnight, the stains never go away.

My father does not take us to any of the popular beaches. He mostly takes us down Carenage by bus. We'd get off just before the bus turns around at the last stop in front of the American base, where a Yankee soldier, dressed in khaki, carries a gun in a white holster like the Lone Ranger in the films at Rialto cinema. I always want to talk to that soldier, ask him about America, where all the men carry guns, but I have to follow my father through a sandy track with overhanging almond trees to a place where huge roots arch into the sea. I once read in a book that there are coconut palm trees along island shores. Tourists pose under them. But I have never seen a coconut palm along this shore.

My sister and I hide behind the bushes when we take off our dresses and our panties. We fold each panty to hide the crotch before we tuck them into our dress pockets. Every time we go to the sea my mother makes sure we wear dresses with pockets for us to hide our underwear. Neither my sister nor I wear brassieres. I'm twelve and she is ten. My tut-tuts are big enough for a brassiere but my mother says she can't buy me one. She says she might be able to afford one by the time I become a young lady. Although she hasn't told me this, I know from my cousin that in addition to the bra, I will also get a set of ten diapers that my mother will make from an old white bedsheet. She'll also give me safety pins to pin the diapers to my panty when I start bleeding. When my blood begins to flow, my father will no longer take me for a sea bath.

My sister and I bathe in grey chambray shorts with red rickrack braid around the thighs that my grandmother has made for us. When we come out from behind the bushes, I cross my arms on my chest to hide my tut-tuts from my father. He thinks I'm acting as if I'm afraid of the water and he tells me to stop being a stupidy.

My sister, whose chest is still flat, hands him our dresses with the panties pushed deep into the pockets, and then he'll tie them together with the white handkerchief in which he has brought leaves from my grandmother, and hang them from a branch of an almond tree. My brother is eleven; almost a man, my father says, so he must behave like a man, so my brother stands out in the open flexing his muscles before peeling off his shirt and pants. He flings them onto the highest root, and wades quickly into the water in his drawers.

He does not go far. He has never liked the sea. The salt turns his eyes red and he can't see for a long time after, but he never tells that to my father. I feel sorry for him but what can I do about it?

My sister and I have to wait until my father slips off his long pants to reveal the short ones he will bathe in. He places his pants and his shirt near my brother's, then he does his exercises. Hands raised above his head, he bends from his waist ten times to touch his toes before breathing deeply. He'll do ten leap frogs, beat his chest, breathe deeply again with his mouth open wide. I wonder if he does this to get rid of his own blight. Only then are we allowed to place our hands in his and walk, one on either side, across the rocks into the sea.

We don't use soap. My father scrubs us with the bush-leaves he has brought – wrapped in the handkerchief – from my grandmother's garden in Bellevue. He says my grandmother has told him that they will help to remove the blight from us. I don't know the names of the scratchy leaves, but they smell like the *cuzaymarho* my mother burns at night to try to get rid of mosquitoes. We always get bitten anyway.

When our knees are deep in the green water, I think how in books the sea is always blue. I have never seen blue sea. I wonder if a blue sea is like the blue my mother soaks white clothes in to make them whiter, or the blue she rubbed on us when we were small to keep jealous people from giving us *mal-yeaux*. I would like to bathe in blue water one day.

The sea floor is slippery. It makes me feel as if I'm standing on a bed of icky moss. I want to move but my father always holds onto me, scrubbing my neck, complaining that my mother does not see to it that we wash our necks clean enough during the week. "That woman is a waste of time," he says. I'd scrunch my toes, and pray silently for him to hurry up so I can try to float, like my sister, who is just out of his reach.

My father has stopped wasting his time with my mother. He left last year. He did not go far, just down the road to Miss Jayne's house.

A few days after my father took his clothes, his sharp knife, and his carpentry tools to Miss Jayne's house, my mother told us, "When you see the lady, you must always say good morning or good afternoon to her. You are not to get involved in big people's business."

My mother always calls her *the lady*, a title I see reserved in books for important people. She'll tell me: "Go by *the lady* and give your father this message", or I might hear her saying to Tante Lill: "He could put toilet in *the lady's* house but he can't put shoes on his children's feet."

One day, just before school started, I saw Miss Jayne walking up the road with a heavy basket on her head. I wanted to duck into Mr. Reggie's parlour to hide until she passed but my feet wouldn't let me. My mother trained us to help women carry load so I took the basket from Miss Jayne and carried it to her front steps. She invited me in for a Solo, calling to my father that I was there. But before he could come from the back, I ran home without stopping.

The following week, when my sister, my brother and I were getting worried that we would have to start school with busted washikongs and raggedy uniforms, Miss Jayne stopped me in the road. She pressed a small brown envelope into my palm. It resembled the ones in which my father received his pay, but I suspected my father did not know about the gift.

"Give that to your Ma," she told me quietly.

When I handed it to my mother and she'd counted the bills, she asked me: "You tell *the lady* thanks?" "Yes," I said. But that wasn't true, and the way my mother looked away from me, I could tell she knew from the sound of my voice I was telling a story. I started feeling bad about it, so later I went to the lady's house to tell her thanks, but my father was in the gallery reading and I turned away before he could spot me.

It was my father's singing I missed most of all. He has a deep voice that sounds like a growl. His songs are mainly about travelling – like Wynken, Blynken and Nod, who sailed off one night in a wooden shoe, sailed on a river of crystal bright, into a sea of blue. He always sang after he and my mother had a row.

I used to tremble every time he came through the house, banging doors, slamming pot covers, or pulling open drawers as he growled about Wynken, Blyken and Nod, or Humpty Dumpty who sat on a wall, or Little Boy Blue who lost his shoe. When he left I missed his singing, but not the rows.

My brother was always a quiet boy with few friends. When my father left he stopped talking altogether. My father said that was my mother's fault but he never explained why.

One Sunday when my father comes to take us to the sea, my brother shakes his head fast, fast.

"Stop shaking your head like a *coonumoonoo*," my father tells him. "Put your foot in your shoes and come on." My brother looks to my mother but she shrugs her shoulders. My father and my mother do not talk. They channel messages through us. My father will say to me, "Ask your mother if she thinks I break a bank", when I've told him that Ma says the electric company is coming to cut out the lights. I can repeat the messages but I have no language that will help me tell my father that I think my brother is afraid of the sea, that maybe he's had a dream, a warning that he should stay away from salt water. But even if I could say such things to my father, he would say that was all the more reason for us to go for a sea bath to wash the blight from all of us.

My brother can't win. He hangs a towel around his neck and I feel like twisting the ends around my own neck, to tie us together, but I can't lift my arms. We are not that kind of family. Besides, my father is hurrying us. We are going to get a ride to the sea in the back of my uncle's truck.

My father sits up front with my uncle. My sister, brother, and I cling to the sides of the small open truck as it swerves around curves on the road to Carenage. My sister says she feels sick. She asks me to knock on the glass partition and beg my father to ask uncle to stop. My father leans out the window and shouts that we are nearly there. Just hold your water. He says we pee too much.

14

We get to the spot where we usually bathe but my uncle keeps going. My father shouts that my uncle knows a better place. A beach with nice sand. We'll get there soon.

We do; faster than we imagined.

The brakes on my uncle's truck come loose and he cannot stop the truck from tumbling down a precipice. My sister and I are pitched into bushes. My father and my uncle manage to leap out, though my uncle breaks an arm. My brother is too frightened to jump. His mouth opens but he does not scream. The truck lands on top of him near some rocks on the beach.

The waves come up from the sea to wash his eyes but they are closed. They leave little flecks like salt on his eyelids.

Later, I hear my father say to my uncle, "What'd I tell you? What'd I tell you? These children blighted!"

BLUE WATERS ARE FOR DROWNING

My mother and Flash were conspiring. From where I sat, five steps above them, bent over my copybooks, I had seen her set the hot iron back onto the flat stone next to the coal-pot, still brimming with hot, ashy balls, before moving to sit next to him on the bench just inside the kitchen door. Minutes before, Flash had come into our house through the front door, a practice he'd begun since his recent return from America.

My mother did not see him stoop to brush his wet lips against my forehead; she did not see me close my eyes as I inhaled the scent of almonds in his hair. It was all too quick, too fleeting.

I lowered my head, pretending to focus on the essay I was supposed to be writing, as he skipped down the steps to my mother. How my ears burned as I tried to listen to them talk, but I heard only whispers.

Two worrying weeks passed before I knew for certain that in their conclave of shushes and inclined shoulders, their bent heads, affirming *uhnnms*, the abrupt silences when I came down to dip a cup of water from the bucket near the back door, that they were deciding my fate – two miserable weeks during which my mother avoided the questions in my eyes, and turned her face away from the words on the tip of my tongue.

To my mother, Flash's re-entry into our lives was a lucky glance from the gods who had abandoned us when my father finally left. Pa had taken off a few times before, only to return, for brief periods, with cracked words, sharp cuffs and drunken spells that left me praying I could find a cure for his unhappiness.

His final departure brought my days at secondary school to an end. After that term, there would be no more money to pay fees, buy my uniform, or my books.

Then came Flash with his suitcase of presents, back from a six-month spell in Dundee, Florida, where he had gone to pick oranges. In his suitcase were small vials of rose cologne for my mother, a dolly for my youngest sister, and two woollen sweaters for me.

Behind my mother's back, he also slipped me a package wrapped in white crepe paper. I hid it in the latrine underneath the pile of old newspapers until I could open it. I found seven shiny panties, one red, one blue, one yellow, one green, one white, one black, one pink, each individually rolled, each with a day of the week embroidered on the right thigh side. Against my cheeks I touched the pink one – Sunday – and its caress was silk. Over the grey chambray pair I was wearing, I tried on the black – for Friday – before rewrapping them all in the crinkled paper. Back in the house, I slipped them into my school bag. It was a few evenings later when he and my mother began their whispering.

Flash had come to our village to work as the watchman on the mango estate at the back of our house when I was twelve. Then, I knew right away that I was going to hate him. With five children and a band of ten to a dozen grandchildren living in our small house, the mango estate was the one place where I found contentment and solitude. I would climb my favourite vert tree from where I could look over the valley to the sea beyond. In my imaginings I saw the waves lashing against the big ships that were taking people from Port-of-Spain, up through the Bocas, beyond Venezuela, past the small islands, bound for New York – to the realization of all my dreams.

When I was younger, I used to dream of England. My brother Mervyn had taken a ship to England five years before, leaving us with promises of dollies and fine English clothes that would make the girls in the village stare at us cokie-eyed with envy. But after the first foreign envelope that contained a brief note about his safe arrival, we heard nothing more from him. Every Christmas, my sisters and I prayed to hear his voice come over the radio when the BBC broadcast greetings from relatives in England. Our prayers were never answered. Later, when I read, in my schoolbook the lament in Charles Kingsley's poem, "The Last Buccaneer", I understood why.

Oh, England is a pleasant place for them that's rich and high;
But England is a cruel place for such poor folks as I...

I imagined my brother in a poor house, just like the children in that Charles Dickens book, so I set my heart on America, where all things were possible.

Near the beach where my father used to take us for a sea bath was the American Military Base, and keeping guard were soldiers who would wink and smile at us. They were from the mysterious land of grand boulevards filled with shops where I would spend the money I would make – after I had sent for my mother and my sisters to live with me in a mansion. Up in my mango tree, my dreams were safe until Flash came to put up a fence around the estate, and a ***Trespassers Will Be Prosecuted*** sign.

From the first day he came into our yard to greet my mother politely – bringing, of course, a basket of calabash, vert, and starch, the sweetest mangoes in the world – from the moment he flashed his gleaming white teeth at my mother, teased her – about what I don't know – to make her laugh so long that she had to wipe happy tears from her eyes, from the minute he opened his mouth to speak to me in that lilting Grenadian accent, a taste to my ear like honey in bush tea, I knew my mother and I were lost.

My mother saved food for him, washed his jeans and white tee-shirts, and on any given evening, as I came round the bend in the road towards our house, her laughter would ripple over me like quiet rain, and I would be grateful to Flash for bringing her out of the place of silence to which she had descended after Pa left.

He was thin and tall, and he smiled so often I used to wonder about the pleasures he must have found in the world. Long nights I spent thinking about him, my ripening teenage body aching for his touch. He must have been twenty years older than me, and he had been places and done things I had only dreamed about. When I thought about him – and it was often – I got so dizzy that, in spite of his permission, I stopped going up the hill out of embarrassment that he would see me shake, and would laugh at the storm passing though a single tree.

When he came by our house in his tight blue dungarees tucked into tall, black boots, a sack over his shoulders with gifts of zaboccas, oranges, cassava, sweet potatoes for my mother – any fruit or ground provision in season on the estate – I was usually bent over my homework. My eyes would dart from difficult algebra problems to his face. He would wink, he would smile, quickly. He was, I knew, reading my heart. We carried on like that for months, with my mother staying up later and later during the picking season to wait for his arrival. I, intent on keeping her company, hoping in quiet desperation for a touch from him, would have willingly propped my eyelids open with small sticks, just to stay awake.

The novel I was reading, *Lady Chatterley's Lover,* only increased my agony.

I had managed to extract it from its hiding place after weeks of hunting it down. Jean, my sister-in-law, had forbidden me to read it, had refused to respond to my questions about the lines she had underlined in red, or why she snapped its covers shut when I approached. I watched her with a vigilance the CIA and KGB would have admired, until one morning, just after she had left for work, I pulled it out from under her mattress.

My fingers parted its worn pages to come to those sentences so carefully underlined, sentences about a woodsman who loved a married woman named Connie, who, a titled Lady though she was, stole away to his small home in the woods to thread the hair at the root of his belly with wild flowers. Forget-me-nots.

My devouring eyes fed on the bold, graphic sentences about sex and love and desire and all the unmentionables that had been consuming me for months. I was so happy that I was not a Catholic like my friend Claudette who would have to confess it all on Saturday to the priest who certainly knew the sound of her voice and would look oddly at her on Sunday when she knelt at the altar for communion.

Lady Chatterley's Lover became my bible.

When Flash took leave to join a group of workers selected to pick oranges in Dundee, I worried that he would slip away from the fields, and disappear in America as other men had been rumoured to do. But just as the mangoes had begun to ripen, he came back. I hummed a calypso as my mother began to laugh again.

He left for Grenada a few days after the week or so of quiet conversations with my mother, and the day after my last day in school my mother told me: "Flash want to talk to you about something important. He leave money for me to buy you the boat ticket." It did not occur to me to question my mother. I could read her eyes.

Under my skirts and bodices in my grip, I tucked the package of panties for each day of the week, minus the one for Saturday, which I put on.

When the boat docked, Flash was not there to greet me. Instead, he had sent a friend named Philip, who, after telling me with a grin that Flash had described me well, said he was to take me in his taxi to Flash's house where I was to wait until he came back from the dentist's. Afraid of throwing up on the boat, I had travelled on an empty stomach but was too embarrassed to tell Philip that I was hungry.

A dizzying drive up a winding road that reminded me of rickrack braid took us far away from the dock and did little to ease the growing pain in my forehead and a grinding in my belly.

Philip stopped his taxi in front of a small wooden house, seasoned black with age, its galvanized roof rusty red. He unlocked the front door to let me into the first of its two rooms, parked my grip next to me, waved, and drove off.

I looked around what was the front room, with two badly varnished Morris chairs and a sideboard of chipped crockery, but saw no signs of food. One of the two doors in the room opened onto the back steps on which a desolate coal pot rested. The other door led me into a room with a small bed, neatly made, and a bureau. On top of this bureau, leaning against a bottle of cologne, were several letters, all airmail, with American stamps, all addressed to Mr. Alton Jordan, Flash's real name. I went back to the front room to sit and wait.

I've often wondered why I did it. Was I angry that, after I had travelled on those rough waters for several hours, up through the swirling Bocas, holding my belly in my hand to come to him, he had not been on the dock to greet me? Was it curiosity about those months he had been away in Dundee, Florida? He had never written to me while he was away, but those letters on top of his bureau were proof that he was communicating with someone from that place. Her name was Agnes. Agnes Jordan. Mrs. Agnes Jordan. He did not have a sister; his mother's name was Lula, and she was dead.

In stories I have read that fingers tremble at such moments. I don't remember mine shaking but I know my heart was racing so fast I felt its rhythm thumping through my chest as I lifted the flap of the first of the letters to read what Flash had already read. Read and saved on top of his bureau, resting against the almond-scent cologne he liked to splash on his neck.

"My darling husband," I read, and my eyes began to water, "I miss you." Six letters, all beginning with "My darling husband, I miss you." Each one had sentences about a baby coming, about loneliness and longing and all the endearments a lover, a real lover like Connie, Lady Chatterley, would say to her woodsman. Words I had spoken to Flash in the dark hollow of my pillow. At what point the tears began to flow, I do not know. Who can remember all that happens at a catastrophic moment, when one's life changes for the worse? I can see myself taking out the panties from my grip, finding a knife in a bowl in the drawing room, and cutting each panty into confetti. I can hear myself screaming, and I can feel a woman and Flash holding my arms. I can hear their voices in a chorus of fear, begging me to stop, stop.

When did the woman leave? How long was it before my screams folded into whimpers? A crippled dog I was, slumped onto the edge of the bed, and Flash was fanning my face with a newspaper and asking what happened, what happened.

The letters at my feet told him, and he rushed into explanations about how much he loved me; that he had wanted me to come to where he was born, not just to see the place, but so he could tell me that yes, he was married, but he didn't love the woman. He had married her only to get his papers so that he could be legal, go to America and send for me, because he loved me. Yes, yes, she was making a baby but he wasn't even sure it was his. She must be trying to tie his foot with that because he had told her he didn't want any children. He wanted me; he wanted me to go to live with him in America. My mother had agreed. What could he do to make me feel better? Did I want to go fishing? He was so sorry he was late but he'd had a dental appointment and the dentist had kept him back. He would borrow Philip's boat the next day so we could fish and he would make me a broth with cascadura, and you know what they say about those who eat the cascadura? They will always come back to the island.

I slept with an ague in my heart in the small bed that night, and he stayed in the front room, on the floor. Mango starch – three of them – awaited me for breakfast but although they were my favourite, and I had eaten nothing since leaving Trinidad, I refused to touch them. The gripes in my belly forced me to accept a cup of tea and a half of hops bread. I ate the food slowly, planning what I would do with every spiteful swallow.

A few hours later we were in Philip's boat and Flash was rowing us over the waves, two fishing poles at our feet. I had said very little to him all morning, only nodding my head when he'd asked if I still wanted to go fishing.

I stared at the water, my heart crying blood, my thoughts hot. Strands of a favourite American song floated through my head: "*Hang down your head, Tom Dooley/Hang down your head and cry/ Hang down your head, Tom Dooley/ Poor boy you gonna die.*" I could actually feel my forehead burning. Flash kept trying to smile away the cut-eyes I was sending him. I hated him. I wanted nothing more to do with him, for I did not believe that a woman, unloved, could have written those letters. How could he have done this to me? To Ma?

An inconsolable sadness settled over me at the thought of my mother. What would I say to her? Without her ever saying as much, I knew that her happiness – and mine – was tied up with my marriage to Flash. Then I thought: how could Ma do this to me? All that whispering. He must have told her he was married. How could she send me out into the blue with nothing to hold on to? The rage I felt toward Flash swelled into a mass that covered her.

The sea turned from green to blue as Flash rowed us away from the shore, and when I thought it was blue enough, I dove into it.

Through the salt water filling my ears I heard No! No! NO! I fought to keep him from lifting me back into the tilting boat, but other arms were grabbing me; men's voices came dimly though the waves, and I opened my eyes to find Flash bending over me on the shore, his hands pressing down on my chest, water flowing down his cheeks.

The next day, before I could turn away from him to walk up the gangplank of the boat that would take me home to Trinidad, he held onto my hands and cried, "You coulda drown. You coulda drown in that blue water. And what I woulda tell your mother?"

I told my mother nothing. All the way back, I had to rub my chest to keep the hurt away from my heart. Perhaps he called her on the telephone in Miss Dorothy's shop before the boat docked in Port-of-Spain, but when I got home, she asked me nothing, and I said nothing. A few weeks later I overheard her telling Jean that Flash had gone back to America for good.

I went to work in a cannery, picking rotten peas out of water. I threw *Lady Chatterley's Lover* into the latrine pit – and lied to my sister-in-law about never touching it. The sound of laughter died in our house.

After a decade of work, I arrived in America. In time, I managed to send for my mother and my sisters to live with me in Michigan.

I had married a man I met on the subway in New York. Perhaps I loved him because he brought me flowers, something no one else had ever done, but love cannot thrive on cuffs and drunken spells, as my mother had learned.

About a month after my divorce, I opened my front door to find Flash standing there, a small bouquet of wilting roses in his hand, and an offer of marriage on his smiling lips.

I thanked him. Said no, and after he had kissed and talked with my mother for a while, making her laughter bounce off the walls, he left.

I never saw him again. I'm certain, though, that my mother knows where he is, for every once in a while I hear her talking conspiratorially to someone on the telephone. She laughs and whispers goodbye when I walk into the room.

THE GIRL FROM BAHIA

(Please sing or hum the first bar of Bob Marley's "No Woman No Cry" before the recitation of this work.)

Yesterday

The girl who came up out of the water was called Suzanna. Soft and young, lovely and tender – in that time when she was called "Suzanna!" by young boys, hard, bamboo shoots, straight with the timbre of desire, limers by the corners of streets with no exits, calling her out of her name when she walked, arms akimbo, sapphires in her toes, in that other time, before she had seen the girl from Ipanema, and fallen in love.

Men saw in Suzanna their hour of redemption. *Oh Suzanna! they cried, Suzanna wait for me.*

Suzanna waited for no man in the time when she was strong and slender, dark and lovely, before she'd slipped into the waters of Bahia to cross the green sea, to see sun worshippers in leather thongs on the beaches of Copacabana, to search for the girl she had seen on the marquee with the dog at her golden heels, sipping Bacardi through ruby-rose lips.

Suzanna told no one that she has come to find the girl from Ipanema, the girl in every carioca's dream.

This is her pilgrimage, as Muslims go to mecca, as Jews to the western wall, as Japanese to Mona Lisa in the Louvre, she has come to Corcovado, walking in the steps of enchantment.

Not once has she asked, *What will I find here? Who asks why there are no houseflies in the Sahel?*

Today

The girl who stands outside the cafe, across from the cathedral of Saint Jude for lost causes, watches soiled waiters flick flies from empty tables and begs with her eyes in a language only the poor can speak. No one answers.

Dry bones, dry bones, no marrow for the worms that will crawl over her wafer-thin bones.

She has walked among oiled bodies on the cream sands of Ipanema, searching for the girl, but no one has said "Ah!"

Lady, Lady have you seen her?

Mister, Mister have you seen her?

Tomorrow

The girl who stands in the shadows on an inside street in Rio has touched the cross on Sugar Loaf mountain, but found no fish, no leaven loaves of bread. She waits for the time when an old man, soft, will call her out of her name, "Sapodilla", and she will suck what little juice is left in his dried up cane.

On the cliffs beneath Rio's Hilton, she has built herself a plastic cave, she heats salt water, she rakes the sand in search of a bread, a coin, a fallen star.

Do you see her?

Lady, lady do you see her?

Mister, mister do you see her?

GLORIA'S SHOP

When Ling Chung first came to Manzanilla, he didn't have a wife. Chinese people don't talk their business but every wind going by carry words, so people soon learned that he had lost his wife to polio. They had one child, a girl, and when he opened his grocery shop by the corner, he hired Gloria, Miss Linzie's daughter, to mind the child for him – this included helping her out with her schoolwork and cooking – and assist him in the shop when the girl was in school.

Gloria had just finished secondary school, but the country's economy was in such bad shape that she was among the thousands of young people with good examination passes who could not get a job. Rather than sit up in her mother's gallery and watch the world go by, she accepted Ling Chung's offer.

This work with Ling Chung pleased Miss Linzie because it was not just a servant girl's position: Gloria would learn the business, and perhaps one day, she would open her own shop.

Ling's shop was, at first, only a little one-door affair, a parlour really, with just three or four shelves of corned beef, condensed milk and Klim; a few barrels of flour, rice, sugar, and pigtails soaking in water, and a box of salt fish. In no time at all, though, the parlour began to expand, and before the end of his first year in Manzanilla, Ling Chung was ordering cement and sand to build a shop with glass windows, a polished wood counter, and a deep freeze to stock Cannings ice cream.

Soon, Manzanillans couldn't buy a single cigarette, they had to buy a whole pack, and their eyes were dazzled by some of the items Ling began to stock, like strawberry jello and American fruits in tins called cocktail. Ah, people smiled, Ling Chung gone more for higher, and they were pleased that, even if they could not

26

all buy the foreign goods, at least one of their own, Gloria, had her hand on them.

They were pleased, too, that there was more than a work relationship between Ling Chung and Gloria. Even the blind could see that Gloria was the madam in the place, for while Christine, the daughter, was in school, Gloria could be seen washing Ling's khaki shorts and hanging them upside down on the line so they could dry quickly; taking charge of the shop when Ling had to go to town on business, keeping a record of who owed what for the groceries they bought on credit, and sometimes demanding payment from some who were slow to pay.

"She acting as if she own the place," some of them grumbled, and some Manzanillans even started saying they were going to "Gloria's shop". One or two macometers reported that once in a while, Gloria did not go home to her mother's house after the shop closed for the night.

Nobody was surprised when Gloria's belly started getting big. What made Manzanilla talk, though, was the fact that she continued to live in her mother's house.

Many of the women were not pleased about this. They understood that a big church wedding would take time, but the least Ling could do, they argued, was to put a ring on the girl's finger. If they were Gloria's mother, *mamayo*, they would go to "the man" in Naparima and put two lights on Ling Chung's head and before you could say by Saint Peter, by Saint Paul, their daughter would have ring on her finger, house, land, store, *tout bagaille!*

The women would lean over the counter and inquire quietly about how Gloria was feeling, and she knew they were not asking only after her physical health. She never complained. Her responses were polite but brief: "I'm feeling well, oui, Miss Melda. Thank you for asking."

This convinced the women even more that Gloria was cutting up inside, and they blamed Miss Linzie for not taking care of the matter.

"Do something for your girlchild," they advised her. "See the woman in Toco. Or go up Naparima. It have a good man up dere. Tie up Ling Chung's foot because you never know with these

Chinese. He will make your daughter into an old woman with a child every five minutes, and then leave her for a wife from China."

Miss Linzie told her neighbours that she had warned Gloria not to get involved with the Chinese man. "I tell her over and over to concentrate on learning the business, but these young girls don't listen to their parents."

Soon, rumours began to spread that Ling Chung's first wife, an Indian girl from Barataria, had not died of polio, but of overwork in childbirth. He would do the same to Gloria. Manzanillans would have liked to show their disapproval by withdrawing their business, but the next nearest shop was six miles away, and back then, only two men in the area owned cars. Bus service was as slow as molasses.

Gloria had a boychild and Manzanillans said thank you Jesus because it was born on a Thursday – when the shop closed half day – otherwise, God knows, the child would have dropped out of Gloria behind the counter. They went to see her at her mother's house and noted that "the child's face cut off Ling Chung's". Ling Chung himself beamed as he offered children free sweet drinks in celebration, and talked to the men about expanding his shop to include a liquor store, the first in the area, and a legacy for his son.

Gloria smiled, but was her usual quiet self through all the fussing and commenting on the child's light skin, straight hair and flat nose – which Miss Tulsie advised would quickly straighten with a daily massage of coconut oil.

Ling Chung established his paternity beyond question when he stood beside Gloria and two neighbours in Saint Margaret's Catholic Church as the child was christened Francis Linzie. This pleased the community since Ling Chung would be listed as father in the church records, even though "illegitimate" would still appear on the birth certificate.

Having gone so far to proclaim his relationship with Gloria, Manzanillans could not comprehend why Ling Chung did not take Gloria and Francis out of Miss Linzie's house. It was what any proper man would do, and they resented him for insulting not only Gloria, but the community as well. "If she's good enough to make a child for him, why she ain't good enough for him to put in a house?"

They watched Gloria under hooded eyes as she took her child in a pram each morning to the shop, and pushed it back down to her mother's house each night. Some of the women tried to tease an answer out of her with questions like, "When you want me to start setting the fruits for the cake, girl?" Or, "You waiting for Ling to build a big house for you, eh? You're right not to move into that chinsy apartment behind the shop."

Gloria would only laugh and shake her head, and gradually, people understood that if she was willing to stand her grind, maybe she knew things that they could not fathom. Maybe Gloria had her head on straight, they consoled themselves, and was holding out for marriage before she moved in. Her neighbours hoped, though, that she was at least getting some money out of the arrangement. And indeed, as Miss Linzie's house expanded with indoor plumbing and a new kitchen, they were consoled that at least Ling was doing something right. Gloria became less of a nine-days wonder.

Interest in her rose again, however, after she had a miscarriage. She had carried the baby, a girl, to about seven months, then began to have violent pains in her stomach. The doctors had warned her to stay off her feet when her ankles started to swell, but she kept right on working behind the counter until one day she had to be rushed away in an ambulance.

She seemed to alter after the loss of the child. Tight lines appeared on her forehead, and the smile that had lit her eyes with a slight mischief disappeared. She rarely joked with the men who were used to a bit of picong in the shop. People whispered that she looked like a picked hibiscus, left to dry up in a vase without water.

By the time her Francis was six, Gloria had gotten pregnant two more times, but both girls were stillborn. And though she seemed as much a part of the shop as the glass case Ling Chung had put in years ago to show off sweetbreads and sugar cakes, she still lived in her mother's house.

Manzanillans, even as they recognized that Gloria was a woman of twenty-three, still faulted Miss Linzie. No good

29

mother, they declared, would sit on her hands while a man took advantage like that. *Go*, they told her. *Go and see the Shango woman in Toco. She will fix Ling Chung*. But if Miss Linzie did anything, it wasn't to Ling Chung. After the last girl child died, Gloria's belly never rose again.

Ling Chung's plan to open his liquor store was being stalled by the head of the Licensing Board in Port-of-Spain. Ling had expanded the shop, built shelves and bought new glasses, but he told Manzanillans that the man wanted a thousand dollars bribe. He would have to sacrifice the new rooms he had intended to put on at the back of the house, he said, to get out of that squeeze. Manzanillans, aware of the opportunistic nature of townpeople, told him a man had to do what a man had to do.

Then early one morning, they saw a large red American car (every big car was American), pull into Ling Chung's sideyard, and when the shop opened, they saw a thin thin Portuguese woman with long black hair down to her waist, rookoo-red lips, and blue eyeshadow, standing behind the counter as if she owned the place. She said her name was Stella and she was Ling Chung's wife.

Manzanilla's mouth fell open. "What we say? What we say? These Chinese men only want to get we daughter's goods, but when it come to owning the shop, they rather put a white woman."

But some people wondered if there was more to the presence of this woman than racial preference, and indeed, they soon found out from Ling that one hand can't clap. The head of the Licensing Board had traded his daughter, a divorcee who had been running wild in clubs all over Port-of-Spain and embarrassing her parents, to Ling Chung. She got an American car as a bonus, and Ling Chung got his rum-shop license – plus a sexy wife to tantalize the men.

Gloria did not go to the shop that day. Sometime that night, Miss Linzie went to have a serious talk with Ling.

She reported that he'd promised to support Francis, but when she'd asked his intentions about Gloria, "He just hang his head like Tom Dooley. He couldn't watch me in the eye self. And you know what the man then tell me? It hurt my belly, I swear it hurt my belly as if it tying up my insides. He say that his wife, yes, his wife taking over the shop, so he will work in the rum shop. He wouldn't need Gloria any more."

From the start it was clear that Stella was no Gloria. She took no care of the books, paid little attention to supplies, and often gave incorrect change to the customers. After parading herself before the men for a few days, she soon got tired with Manzanilla, and every day she put on her halter top and shorty shorts, jumped in her car, and went speeding down the road with a beach blanket in the backseat.

Parents complained to Ling that his wife never looked right nor left when she was driving. They were afraid for their boys to play cricket or football in the road; they feared having to send their children to the standpipe for water, or even to his shop for small items because they never knew when this woman's car would spit gravel in their faces, and cause them to leap into the canal.

One or two of the women tried talking to Stella; it was the fashion to talk a problem over peacefully for the betterment of the community. But she turned her back on them and flounced off. While they blamed Ling for bringing "this cross" to the area, they understood how little control he had over her. After all, they said, "She was a wajang woman from behind the Bridge. If she own father couldn't handle she, what you tink Ling could do?" They even began to feel a little sorry for him.

About two months after she'd arrived, Stella ran over Mister Graves's dog. Everybody knew the dog. They called him Cripple because one of his hind legs was shorter than the other, and he dragged himself about. Even the postman slowed down his bicycle for Cripple to pass across in front of him. But Stella came pelting down the road one morning and hit the dog, bam! To make matters worse, she righted the car and sped on. When Ling Chung later tried to give Mister Graves some money, Mister Graves spat on the ground in front of him and turned away without accepting it.

Some of the neighbours complained to Gloria, not so much because they expected her to be able to do anything, but so she would know that they empathized with her, that now they too

31

were being persecuted by this "Potogee blight"; they knew how she must be feeling.

Gloria listened to their complaints with only a few murmurs, a nod of her head, and a laugh when the women suggested that Ling must certainly be regretting his decision. "He eating the bread the devil knead in truth," they said.

Gloria had taken up sewing, a trade she had wisely learned in school. She bought a Singer, installed it in her mother's front room, and began sewing fancy clothes for the young girls in the area. She devoted her time to her sewing and to Francis, ignoring the overtures of several of the young men who now envisioned opportunities for liaisons. Rebuffed, these young men claimed that she had quailed up inside, that she had allowed the Chinese man to suck her dry, and some women said it was true, only a woman who was suffering from severe *tabanka* could be so icy.

If Gloria heard these comments, she paid them no obvious attention. Even when word floated out that Stella had told Ling Chung to stop paying for Francis' schooling, Gloria did not, as people fully expected any woman to do, go up to the store, push her hand in Stella's face, and make a big bacchanal. Some Manzanillans wondered why Gloria did not leave the district, start over, make a new life for herself and her son, but others admired her stoicism in the face of a man who had shamed her.

With Stella sporting, Ling Chung took Christine, only thirteen, out of school to sell in the store while he worked in the rum shop. Christine, who had grown fond of Gloria, often came to visit, and she too complained of having to cope with the store, the housework and the "potogee" woman.

"Can you talk to Daddy?" she begged, but Gloria explained that she and Ling had not exchanged two words since Stella's arrival.

"Your father didn't tell me what he was going to do," she said. "He put himself into that mess and he has to suffer for it."

"But I'm the one who's suffering!" Christine moaned. "I'm the one who had to give up school. I'm the one tied to a shop counter for the rest of my life."

Gloria shook her head and advised the child to make the best of her situation, but a week later when Christine had to be rushed to the clinic after a hot pot of water spilled from the stove onto her leg, and Stella wasn't even in the house to help, Gloria went to the store to talk to Ling. Whatever she said made no difference because Stella continued to run the streets, while Christine, her leg bandaged, worked in the shop all day.

One foreday morning, not long after that, Gloria got up, gave Francis his breakfast, made him dress in his best white shirt and black pants, and walked with him down to the bus stop. She carried a heavy bag in one hand, and with the other, she gripped her son's arm. Miss Linzie watched them go from her gallery. She didn't wave. Her neighbours made the sign of the cross to bless this day Gloria had finally come to her senses.

Gloria and Francis came back late that afternoon, just as the streetlight came on, when most people were inside having their tea. Gloria held Francis's right hand while he carried the now empty bag in his left. As they walked slowly up the centre of the road, some of the neighbours who had seen them leave, watched with their mouths open in such surprise they couldn't say a word.

Why had she changed her mind, they wondered. Where was she coming from? What had she been doing all day with Francis? Maybe she had gone to put Ling in court for not supporting the boy. Some of them reminded themselves that a quiet woman is a dangerous woman, and although Gloria had shown that she had more guts than a calabash, even a calabash could burst open. They watched her and the boy closely as the two of them walked up the road slowly, not looking left or right.

A horn suddenly blasted, and Stella's car came up the road from the beach, tires crunching. Gloria and her son kept walking in the middle of the road as if they owned it. Just as they rounded the corner, Gloria released Francis' hand, rubbed the top of his head with something she had taken from the bag, and stepped into the canal, leaving the boy standing still in the middle of the road, holding the bag and with the street light shining over him.

Stella, coming round the bend, realized at the last minute that the child was not going to jump aside. She swerved the car, barely missing Francis. The car hit the lamppost, and she jerked over the steering wheel as the post cracked and electric wires fell.

Neighbours dashed out to help, but there was little they could do with electric wires lying dangerously on the ground. They had to wait for the fire brigade to arrive, their attention riveted to the woman in the car. Hardly anyone noticed that Gloria had lifted her son up to her chest and was carrying him like a baby into Miss Linzie's yard.

Stella lost both legs, and when she left the hospital, she went back to Port-of-Spain. Manzanillans expressed their sympathies to Ling Chung by trusting more goods than ever, as they waited expectantly for Gloria to move back into the shop.

They were surprised when she did not. Christine asked her, and even Ling Chung had the audacity to plead his case with her, promising, Miss Linzie reported, to make her a partner in the shop. But Gloria continued her sewing business, and within a year, she opened a small grocery in Miss Linzie's front yard.

Maybe because her prices were always a few cents lower than Ling Chung's, or maybe it was because she took to selling a few cigarettes if a customer could not afford a pack, and a pound of rice instead of a prepackaged bag, and fresh mangoes and bananas and grapefruits and oranges, instead of dyed cherries in a tin can, and corn flakes in a box, maybe it was because she was one of them, and they were proud to send their children to buy from Gloria's shop, Manzanillans patronized her store and neglected Ling's.

Ling's business grew worse when Stella's father refused to approve a renewal of his liquor license, and in no time he was forced to close down. He soon left Manzanilla, and some people said he had gone to Canada with Christine, but he really went to another village called Rosehill.

Gloria gave up sewing to concentrate on building up her business, and by the time Francis started secondary school, she had her own rum shop and grocery store. She has not married, but she's still a young woman and every now and then, she will make a nice dress for herself, and go to a fete in San Fernando. Young men lean against the walls, cigarettes dangling from their lips, saliva dripping from their mouths at the prospect of being in the bamboo with Gloria, but to this day she dances alone.

HOMELESS IN O'AHU

In the valley of the temples a woman grates pineapple with her teeth. She spits, but brown fragments still nestle in crevices between chalk stumps in her slack jaws. Dancing her tongue from left to right, up and down against the cracked silver that used to fill her holes, she bruises the tip. Blood squirts her gums, but that pain is small measured to the one she lives. Long ago she lost her molars, her four pillars of wisdom, in a dog fight. She has made sawdust of crowns and caps and fillings in her longing to return to dust.

At dawn, mist in the valley hangs about her like a first communion veil. Her eyes are wet with dew. She washes her neck, her armpits, with drops the broad-back eddoe leaves have saved for her; she has always been a modest woman. Her name is Crystal and her son has sent her to live in this kingdom of O'ahu. Some days she wants to fling herself off the Pali, dive to the plains, sing with warriors on the way down, but a hand always grabs her, just at the last moment.

In another time she owned sixty white chickens, gifts from her husband on the twenty-fifth anniversary of their coupled life. They lived then on the San Andreas Fault and she knew the chickens were his penance. She loved them anyway, and fed them each morning with leftover food from the night before. In the doorway of their highwire coop she sprinkled grains of boiled brown rice and loops of cold spaghetti, like the Pope at the Vatican blessing the crowds on Easter Sunday. They died but did not rise again. At night they clawed across her brain, pecking at her cells until her son came to bandage her head in white.

But that was after – after her husband had ridden into Carlsbad on his bicycle made for two to break the glass windows of the new

35

post office, to pelt the new supervisor with rocks, to throw the grenade he had kept in the garage among his souvenirs from My Lai. The newspapers said: sometimes the brain explodes.

When the sun turns south over Mamala Bay, Crystal is waiting. She likes the windward side where the rain gods pee. In a twisted aluminium chair beneath a pine tree at Waimanalo, she waits for lightning to strike. Even if her eyes are closed, she wants to know when it happens, so into the pleats of flesh around her throat she has folded foil to improve the reception. On good days she wears red, and crowns her hair with anthuriums. She saw an angel once, down on the docks, hanging from the bow of a ship. How she would love to be that angel, long yellow hair floating on the wind. Sometimes, as a gale crosses to the sea, Crystal dances like Salome. She makes her wish, a small one, but even the elves of Waimea Canyon, to whom she has offered nine novenas, have been silent.

After the incident at Carlsbad, their only son, Harvard '84, teaching philosophy at Princeton, declared he was adopted. He refused to visit his father in the pen, but wrote long letters to *The Nation* on behalf of political prisoners in Iran. It was he who sent Crystal to Hawaii, to live in a kitchenette in Waikiki. But the room was claustrophobic and one evening a voice from the sea called her. No one has seen her since. They don't know how to look. Crystal is on the beach at Waimanalo, trying to recall with precision when she took her first step toward cataclysm.

She can remember old rhymes: *Tuesday's child is full of grace… Humpty Dumpty sat on a wall… Wynken, Blynken and Nod one night sailed off in a wooden shoe*, but she does not know why she has written PRAY on a piece of cardboard and pinned it to her chair. She remembers climbing a thousand steps to Koko Head, but not coming down again, and she knows she once dove into the rocks at Ewa Beach, but was it the Samoan who fished her out, who caked her broken temples with black mud until she could think again?

On a day when the sky is grey, she looks up and sees a rainbow over Hawaii Kai. She must kiss it so she pushes her cart from Waimanalo to Sea Life Park, east to the rainbow's end where she can taste yellow and green and orange. She has already swallowed red and blue. The sea is rough on the north shore. Big rocks stand in her way. Still she pushes on. The sun is coming to suck her colour. Push, push, push, Crystal. Her cart rattles over stones to the end of the world.

THE STONE GROWER

My grandmother knew, the moment she set foot on the land, that she could make the stones grow. The old lady beside her must have seen her back stiffen, her fingers ball up tight-tight under her knuckles, her jaw set hard against doubt, for she issued, for the third time since they had met at the junction, the warning that: "This land blighted, Miss Lady. I don't know why Mister Brunton trying to rent it out. He knows good and well the land blighted."

"I am taking it," Granny told her. "You say it costing fifteen dollars a year? That includes the water rate?"

A jagged laugh broke through the old lady's lips. "Water rate? What water rate? You see any pipes coming up the track? You see any standpipe in the road? As far as the government's concerned, this valley is behind God's back. Me and my grandchildren will dead before they pipe water up here. You have to use the spring."

"And how far that is?" My grandmother spoke as if she had already paid the land rent, as if this was the moment when the land became hers. Leading the old lady back to the road, she had bent down to lift a big stone out of her way, to clear a path through the rocks.

"You have children?" The old woman stepped after my grandmother, conceding leadership to this woman she must have thought had some mad blood flowing to her head, oui, because is only a mad woman would want to come and live in a quarry. She musta born wrongsided.

Bending down, rising up, flinging a stone here, another one there, my grandmother wasn't even breathing hard, though she had to lean from her knees because of the full belly she was carrying. "Eleven, and this next one on the way," she told the old lady.

"Well, that is a good thing," the old lady nodded. "You going to need them to tote the water from the spring. It's up the hill." And she pointed high with the bent guava stick that aided her slow progress.

My grandmother's eyes followed the point of the stick to the mountain full of bush and deep trees rising behind this strange piece of land on which not a plant, not a fruit tree, not a blade of grass was growing. And if she wondered how she was going to make the stones grow, she kept it to herself.

"Down below is a ravine," the old lady added. "But in this dry season is only a trickle. Rainy season, though, water come down the hill so hard you could catch crab to eat for days."

"So if the water not flowing down to the ravine, it must have a pool under the spring, eh?" Granny was already calculating how far she and her children would have to walk to gather the water required for mixing the cement for the concrete they would pour to make the flooring for the little house she had in mind.

"Nylon Pool," the old lady's face wrinkled into a smile again. "That's what we name it. Clear clear sweet water. You could see your face in it. Deep too, though. They say jumbie living in the rocks there but I never see none."

If she heard the warning note about jumbies my grandmother didn't flinch. She was too busy calculating: a ravine with sand; a pool with clear water; stones to bolster the foundations. She could have a place to rest her head. She could stop moving from *hacket* to *packet* with her children, begging a lodging from this sister, this cousin, this uncle.

She signed the paper promising to pay Mister Brunton, the estate owner, three dollars five times a year to live on a piece of land that didn't have a tree, a plant, a bush; only rockstones in the dirt. Not even moss able to settle on them.

"She brain addled, oui," the old lady had whispered to Mr. Brunton when they had returned to his house. "I tell her. I warn her. I don't want my conscience to bother me in my old age. But she insist. I tell you is madness we seeing."

But this old lady didn't know Ma Cumberbatch; didn't know that she came from a long long line of Cumberbatch women who had scratched their way like fowls out of Anguilla village when

Indians came to work the cane, women who had crossed the Caroni River, weighed down with babies riding their hips, bands strapped to their backs, bundles of food and wares on their heads, mud sticking between their bare toes, walking for miles in the hot sun, heels twisting, soles getting tough like goatskin, their dress-tails tied up in knots above knees rough like graters from kneeling so long in the fields where they had planted cane. For what? Nothing. For whom? Not for themselves. So what now was a few rockstones, eh? What now was a quarry compared to the barrack-yard where she and nine of her eleven children had been given refuge in a two-by-four behind the house her sister was renting from the people who lived in Champfleurs where she worked seven days a week in their kitchen, glad to get the gizzards and feet from the chickens to bring home to boil down with salt and bird pepper so all of them could go to sleep with their belly full, even if it was for one night only, praise God.

She would gather her sons from the four corners of Trinidad where she had parcelled them out for survival. Get Maxie, her oldest, from his godfather's house in Saint James, get Lennox, from his Uncle Amby's place in Arouca where she'd had to put him after they were forced to move from the house in Tranquillity when Papa died. Papa – her husband since he was sixteen and she was fifteen. Crossing the road from the *Hotel Normandie* where he worked as a bartender, drunk, the police say, too blind drunk and too disorderly to see the car coming round the Savannah. Dead on the spot. But you can't blame the car! How you going to blame the car? The man should have watched where he was going. What insurance? Lodge benefits? He stopped going to Lodge years ago. Miss Lady, here, take these few dollars the waiters at the hotel scraped together. It's better than nothing.

My grandmother took in washing: linens from the *Hotel Normandie*, clothes from their long-staying guests; nurses' uniforms and policemen's shirts.

"It was your mother," she would tell me later. "Your mother kicking me in my belly, biting the navel string, trying to tell me she didn't want to be born in no barrack-yard. She was the first one born on this land."

And sitting up with her on the ironing nights that stretched towards morning, with her pressing pleats into the skirts of uniforms for nurses at the General Hospital, I would beg her to tell me the story of how she made stones grow and how she had built the house. She would speak about the house – "Two, really, because the first one fall down, galvanize cutting Maxie in his forehead. That's why he has that V in the centre" – but not the stones.

"But why?" I would ask again and again. "Why nothing couldn't grow on this land. Why?"

And it took her years to tell me, years to answer, because she didn't want me to get frightened. I was a sickly child, born with blood running from my nose, and fear could bring on the sickness.

But after she saw I could walk home from Belleview in the dark by myself, with jumbiebirds hooting, dogs crying and, worst of all, cats jumping out at me from the bush; when she saw that I didn't bolt like my sisters from the phantom in Miss Oya's yard, when I didn't come crying about hairs standing up on my head and my blood running cold, then she told me:

"Because is here they kill the priest. The land blight from that time. From the day they find the priest's body, every green thing on the land die. They say it would take a miracle to get anything to grow here again. I didn't know that. I come from Saint James and nobody tell me about the priest until I start to put up my little house. Is then I hear the story. They say the priest was friending with Mister Brunton's wife. Not the present day Mister Brunton. His great-grandfather. God forgive me, I only repeating what people say because it was long before my time. They say old Mister Brunton was the priest's friend – I always warning you about calling people friend. Friend will take you but they won't bring you back. He thought the priest was his friend, inviting him over to his house, giving him money to build the church, when all the time they say the priest was friending with Missis Brunton, so people say. But old Mister Brunton was the last to know. One day he tell his wife he was going to visit his sugar mill in Arouca. Back then it take a long time, sometimes a whole day, to ride from this Valley to Arouca, so she didn't expect him back for two days.

When the mark buss, old Mister Brunton come back early and hide in the back of a tall press. Is so he come to know why people was always laughing behind his back. A few nights later, he arrange to meet the priest on this land. He tell the priest that the Yorubas was going to meet here to plan a revolt. Back then people still in bondage, you know, and even the priests in league with the estate owners to keep them down. Morning after, Mister Lezama passing through the land to get to his garden up the hill before cocks crow and what he see but the priest's body lying in blood near his donkey, and the donkey eating grass cool cool. Police arrest the top man in the Yorubas, but then they find out they had the wrong man. A boy come forward to say how Old Mister Brunton give him a piece of paper to take to the priest, and you know how some children fast fast, the boy read the note – they say old Mister Brunton didn't know he could read. Poor man, he hang himself. People say it would take a miracle to clean this land. They say nothing except stones would ever grow here."

"But how come we have mango, cashew, breadfruit, and zabocca growing in the yard?" I always asked this, even though I knew the answer.

She would place the iron back on top the pot of burning coals, take up a lily-white shirt, sprinkle it with warm water, lay it out on the table, and before she took up the pad to reach for the hot iron again, she would shake her head at me, smile, and begin the litany, "Child, how much times you want me to tell you the same story? I tell you I come from a long line of women from Africa."

"Last time you say the women come from Anguilla village. Now you say Africa. Which one is true?"

With her free hand she tapped me on the forehead. "So what you think? You think we just drop from the sky into Anguilla village? No, child, we come from Africa. Now let me tell the story and don't interrupt me again or I sending you to bed.

"I come from a long long line of Yoruba women. We know how to do things. We know how to fix the land to make stones grow. After the first house fall down, and I hear the story about the priest's blood, I bring your Tante Lill and some other women, and we wash the land and bless the place."

Slowly, repeating the names so they would be engraved in my brain, she would describe the roots and herbs they had used.

Sometimes, just to tease her, I would say I didn't believe the story, and she would ask, "How you think we survive on this island so long? Is we who had to drink salt water to keep from dying in those ships that was bringing us from overseas to set we down in the cane fields in Anguilla village to grow sugar on we knees. Yes, child. We cross the Caroni barefoot with children on we hips, babies on we backs, bundles of wares on we head. Some of we didn't have a man to depend on. But that didn't keep we from moving from Perseverance to Tranquillity. Who could slow down to catch a breath? Who could stop to hear herself think? Not we. We come without much, but we come with plenty."

Until I left my mother's house to go overseas, Granny continued to tell me the story of the long line of strong women in our family, each time adding a little bit more, like brown sugar to make sorrel sweet.

BUSH DREAMS

ONE

"Ma," I screamed from the gallery. "The postman has a letter for you."

My mother, bending over to dry her soapy hands on the hem of her skirt, came slowly to the front of our house. Carefully, as if a stranger was handing her a rose, she took the white envelope with its red and blue stripes from the postman.

"It's from overseas," he announced, as if we were too blind to see that it was an airmail envelope. "But it doesn't say who send it." Sitting halfway upon his bicycle seat, the cuffs of his khaki pants clipped about his ankles, one foot on the ground, the other on the pedal, he waited for my mother to reveal the letter's identity, as I, excitement dribbling down to my toes, hopped around her.

"Who write; Ma? Velma? It's from Velma, right Ma?" On my way to the latrine I had heard the postman's bell, and had dashed to the front yard. But he had refused to give me the letter.

"Is for your mother. I have to put it in her hand. You see there? You could read that?" He held the letter away from my face the way I held bread away from the dog. I couldn't reach it but I could read "To Mrs. Carmen Phillips only." The "only" was underlined three times.

"Call your Ma," he had commanded me.

I could feel the urine that I had not had a chance to get rid off. I could feel the weight of it, hot, pressing down, but I tightened my thighs to squeeze it back up into my belly.

My discomfort grew as my mother stood, silently holding the letter as if the wonder of it would never cease. She braced against the gate while between her right thumb and forefinger she held the envelope, half drooping, as if she wasn't sure if she should keep it or allow the breeze to blow it away.

"Ma," I pulled on her arm. "Open it. Let me open it for you, please." But she ignored me. Instead, she turned the letter over, to read her name and our address: *Pole Number 69, Rich Plain Road, Trinidad, West Indies*, scrawled in blue ink, Velma's favourite colour. As if to reassure herself that the letter was really hers, my mother ran her fingers over the lettering.

"It leave New York since last month," the postman told her. "But with the go-slow, nuh, it just reach the post office. I say to mehself, since it's Friday, let me bring it up for you."

I wished he would ride away. I wanted to say to him, "Leave my mother and me in peace, nuh. Get on with your job." But that would be rude. Even at age ten, I was still considered a child who must keep a high fence between myself and big people.

The postman said expectantly, "Well, I hope is good news?" My mother did not appear to have heard him. He coughed. Still, my mother did not respond. He looked up the road to where Miss Kelton waited at her gate, her arms akimbo, signifying her impatience with a slight wave of annoyance.

He sucked his teeth and said, "Well I gone, oui. Is the government work I have to do." Then cutting his eyes from my mother to me, he warned, "Beg water never boil cow skin, chile," before rising up on his pedals to power himself up the road.

He was right. I knew my mother. The more I begged, the less likely she was to let me read the letter, but I was getting impatient with her silence. Couldn't she see I was holding strain? Couldn't she tell I wanted, badly, to pee?

I said, "You going to stand there till cock get teeth?"

Clearly, she was in a different world. She had to be. In our world, she would never allow me to get away with speaking to her like that. There we were, standing in the same space, in the same time, yet she had gone away. Drifting like my kite, the one that had flown away from me the day before, leaving me with empty hands, wondering if it would land or get tangled up in a tree.

I wanted to grab the envelope from her. I wanted to slit the flap open with my big thumb, to read what my sister had written at long last, two years after she had left for America. Nearly two years since I had thought she was dead.

My mother ran her fingertips over the writing again, over the four stamps with a black circle of notes and numbers impressed upon them, then along the red and blue stripes that resembled a flag, and as she did so, she smiled.

"Open it, nuh, come on. Is from Velma? Eh? Eh? Ma... a... a!"

It was then she heard me, only then, because I bawled out the way I used to bawl in the middle of the night when the bad dreams came over me. She looked down in surprise. "What you still doing here, chile? Go next door and ask Miss Joseph if she has some blue for me to put in the clothes?" She shooed me away as if I was some stray fowl, and I knew she must be going mad because she would never, ever, beg Miss Joseph even for a grain of salt.

"But I want to see the letter. Can I touch it? Why're you being so stingy?" I knew, even as the words slipped out, that I had gone overboard.

"The onliest thing you going to feel this morning, young lady, is my hand on your behind. Do what I say. Now!" I backed away, but I saw her unlocking the hook and eye in her bodice. I saw her pushing the letter into her brassiere, then locking back the hook, before returning to the washtub.

Just as if a lightening bolt hadn't fallen from the sky, my mother bent over the tub, picked up my father's pants, and began to rub it against the jucking board, all the time staring down at the dirty water.

Vexed, I stayed in the front yard to kick the roots of the guava tree, to bust up the sole of the last pair of school shoes I owned. I picked up a stone to pelt down a green guava; I bit it, and spat the hard pieces at the chickens. I chased a dog in heat from our gate. I broke a stick from the mango vert tree and started digging a hole in the ground like dogs do when they are searching for something. I just started digging that hole, digging that hole, flinging the dirt away with my bare hands and digging out more until something started squeezing my insides and I could feel the water coming because I knew that letter was from Velma and I was getting frightened. I didn't even realize I was peeing until the water started coursing down my thighs onto my white washikongs.

Ashamed, I thought of other things, other reasons for my suffering as I uncrossed my legs and slunk awkwardly toward the latrine.

TWO

Two a.m. my mother woke up screaming. My room is right next door to hers so I could hear everything. I heard my father rolling over and asking her what she was bawling out so for. I heard her saying something in a dream had frightened her. I heard my father telling her that he might as well not come anymore because, lately, she's been waking him up with her bad dreams and it takes him a long time to fall back asleep. My father comes some nights to sleep in my mother's bed. I have heard my mother say to him, "You come. You come, eh? The lady must be gone Tobago."

I heard my mother go to the kitchen and I heard when she came back to sit on the edge of the bed where the springs squeak. I knew she was holding a wet cloth against her forehead because that is what she does in times like these. She bands her head with a wet cloth, and sometimes, she mourns. When she mourns, I hug a pillow to my ears.

I heard my father grinding his teeth. I heard my mother sigh as she lay back down and tried to pull, gently, a part of the cover my father wrapped himself into.

I know my mother didn't go back to sleep because I stayed awake until the cocks began to crow. She went into the kitchen to knead the flour for my father's bake, and to heat a pot of water to take the chill off the cold water in the bucket near the back steps where he bathes.

THREE

My father did not want Velma to go away. He and my mother argued about it night and day. He said America was a rotten-down place where Black people were worse off than the people who lived in Shantytown near the rubbish heap we call Labasse. My mother said if that was so, then how come Christabella, Mr. Joseph's daughter, made so much money in America that she could build her father a concrete house and send for him to come on holiday? My father said the Josephs would sell their souls to the devil for a shilling, and who knows what Christabella was doing in America. She was always too hot for her own good anyway. Besides, how come my mother preferred to listen to other people instead of to her own husband? He should know. Hadn't he been to America in 1960 to pick fruits in Florida? Given up his good good job with Road Works to run behind the Yankee dollar?

"I wish Florida would break off and fall under the sea. If you see where we sleep. Ten of us have to sleep in a shack. Every morning we have to jump up early early to go to pick oranges. Orange? The juice make me throw up. If I ever see a Yankee orange again in my life I will turn beast. All day in the hot sun filling up baskets, filling up trucks. Night-time? Night-time we glad to crawl in a corner to get a few hours shut-eye before the bossman come breaking down the door for us to go in the field again. Moon and sun fighting in the sky and we in the groves, picking fruit. Three months we stay up there and is only when it was time to come back home that they let we go into the city. But you know what? Hear this. The boss man keep back we passports, in case some of we would get away, and stay in America. Stay in America? Who want to stay in that place?"

"But it's not that way in New York," my mother says quietly. "I hear New York is a good place."

"New York? New York?" My father's voice begins the furious bubble of boiling water. "Who wants to go New York? Can't even see the damn sea. Only a bunch of tall-arse buildings blocking the breeze."

By now, my father's voice is thunder rolling along the rim of the hymn my mother is singing, just under her breath: "*Oh God, my strength in ages past. My hope for years to come…*"

"What I want to send my daughter up there for? No! Let Velma stay here. Let her go and learn to sew by Miss Ivy. Seamstress is a good trade. Let her learn to sew."

Later, I heard my mother telling Velma not to mind what my father was saying. He's just worried for her. She will talk to him again. But once she realized he wasn't going to change his mind, she stopped arguing. She took in more ironing. She cooked food and sold it to the men paving the Dry River. She baked and sold wedding cakes, pasting on thick white frosting with a flat knife on which she rubbed lime. I stayed up in the long nights to watch her squeeze pink rosettes around the sides of the bride's cake, and red around the groom's. She scrimped and saved, and threw two susu hands that my father did not know about. She cheated herself, buying only three small slices of carite or red fish from the van, one piece for my father, just in case he came that week, one for Velma to give her strength, one to split between the rest of us. She would eat a little curry sauce on her rice, sitting on the back steps, her dress forming a basket between her knees.

At night she washed our socks and our school uniforms, hanging them behind the fridge to dry because we owned only one set. She stayed in the latrine too long sometimes, counting what she had saved, then rewrapping the dollars, the shillings, the cents, wrapping them back up in newspaper before pushing it down into an old biscuit tin that fitted in a hole underneath her washtub.

I had to bide my time, to wait and watch until I could thief a chance, but I always knew how much was in the tin. I also knew that not long after it was empty, Velma would be gone.

If my father guessed what she was doing, he said nothing, but his silences were loud. Out of the blue he would make us turn over our mattresses and shake out our pillowcases. The rafters shook after he searched under each pot, pan, and bottle.

He would come home unexpectedly when my mother was away and I watched through a chink in the door as he searched her bureau drawers. He stopped giving her money. Instead, he set up an account in the shop against which she could trust food, nothing else. Then he stopped coming home every night. He came on Fridays though, to bring his dirty clothes, and to pick up the clean ones. And on those nights I watched him and my mother circle each other like gamecocks in a ring, pecking, parrying, just waiting for an opening to dive in for the kill.

49

Many days I wished I had a big brother. A brother I could lean against; a brother who would throw me up and catch me before I fall. Instead, I had three sisters and three brothers who were gone – Mervyn to England and Noel to Tobago. I try not to think about Gary, my brother who died. Sometimes I see him in my dreams. I call out, but he doesn't answer.

Velma was the oldest girl, then came Jenna, four years older than me, and Camille, two years younger. Velma was always drawing in her notebooks, colouring with coals or pencils, staining her fingers with roukoo, shoe polish, or dye she made from plants because she didn't have watercolours or brushes to paint dark faces, blue hills, white skies, or silver rain falling on the galvanize.

When my mother took us to the zoo, she let Velma sit off by herself on a bench to sketch giraffes while we went around to see all the other animals in their cages. Velma liked the animals but she hated the zoo. She said one day she was going to Africa, to see real animals running free.

One Saturday, the dam in my father broke loose. He burned Velma's sketch books after he came home unexpectedly to find her sitting in front the fowl run, drawing chickens, the yard he had told her to sweep, still dirty. He told my mother he didn't know how else to make the girl understand that she had to do something constructive with her life.

"When you're poor in this world," he said, "you have life hard as it is. When you're poor and deaf too, why try to make it harder? Why get involved with things that only belong to rich people?"

My mother bit on her lips, but I could see her jaws trembling. Velma signed furiously as she stamped on the ground before running inside. Later, I heard my mother telling my father that maybe, just maybe, God gave Velma the talent to draw and paint to make up for not giving her good hearing.

I had to wait all that day to know what was in the letter. That evening, my mother and I sat, as usual, on the back steps watching corns roast over the coal pot. On other nights I would have been catching candleflies in a jam bottle with the boys next door, but tonight, I sat between my mother's knees, waiting for her to open Velma's letter.

"She's doing all right," my mother assured me. "She's doing just fine, praise God. I know he didn't send her up there to fail." She read softly to herself, then told me what Velma had written, not just to her, but to me and Camille as well.

She told us about trains running under the earth, and how frightened she was until they stopped and she could climb out into the fresh air. She asked us to imagine Carnival was every day because that was how New York looked, with thousands of people on the streets, morning, noon and night. She said she got a job with a singer named Nina Simone, and Nina took her to a doctor to see about her hearing. She said the doctor gave her something to wear in her ears and now she could hear much, much better. Of all the sounds she was hearing, she liked to listen to water running because it reminded her of the spring behind our house.

She was going to get a chance to travel to California when Nina went on the Johnny Carson show. She said she wished we had television so we could see the Johnny Carson show on the night Nina would be on, but since we didn't own one, she drew a picture of Nina in front of a microphone in a long, tight fitting dress, with a box around her to represent a television. "I will try to send down a small TV for you all for Christmas," my mother read aloud, then blew her nose as water fell from her face. I could tell by the tinkling sound she made that she wasn't crying from sadness.

Just before she sent me to brush the corn from my teeth, she rumpled my hair. "All I ever wanted was for you all to know your dreams don't have to stay in the bush," she said. "I feel sorry for your father because no matter how hard I try, I can't get him to understand that."

SNAKES

When my mother was in her late fifties and I was old enough to remember fear, a woman wise beyond our seasons told her that she would die from a snake's bite. Around this woman's right wrist was tattooed a ring of tiger wire, the sign of her indenture, and in her face were deep gorges of age. As a girl, she had come from India across rough waters to Trinidad to work in the cane fields of Couva.

With startling exactness, she could recall the number of cane crops she had helped to harvest, the dates of her children's births, the village and family she had left in Uttar Pradesh, and what she was doing on the night a neighbour cut her husband's throat. If only her husband had listened to her. A widow, she had come to make a new life out of ashes.

She taught my mother how to use thistle to increase the amount of milk in her breasts after my brother Gary was born, and it was she who had mixed up the portion of cocoa butter and aloes that saved my uncle's toes after a scorpion's bite.

My mother relayed this prophecy of her death with some lightness, pleased, I suspected, that it contradicted her own suspicion that she would die of pleurisy, a fate her own mother suffered after being drenched in dew.

My grandmother died far too young. She had ironed too long over hot coals. Walking home in the small hours of the morning, head uncovered, she had caught a cold, then fever, then pleurisy, and at fifty-eight, she was dead.

Terrified at the thought of my mother's death, I guarded her closely, giving up my interest in boys – with whom I played hide-and-seek; fighting sleep – wishing I could prop open my eyes to watch her as she pressed clothes until two or three in the morning.

Sleep would eventually overcome my vigilance, and my mother would place the iron on a pad so she could carry me to my cot.

These were the days before we had electricity, before my cousin Earl had finished his electrician's apprenticeship that taught him how to tap the current from the lamp pole in the street to give up free lights.

Day after day I would run home after school, shouting for my mother as I rounded the bend by Miss Dorothy's shop, frantic when I didn't see her bending over the washtub in the yard, hanging clothes on the line, shelling peas on the back steps, or doing any of the million and one jobs that kept her on her feet all day.

Our house had no ceiling, and I would lie awake some nights, uneasy, my eyes raking the rafters, searching for a slither, a shadow of the snake I sensed must live in our house, waiting, biding its time to kill my mother. I planned and plotted to cheat it. I would go away. I would send for my mother. I would go to New York where there were no snakes, where there was no bush for them to crawl from.

But how to overcome a major obstacle: my mother's oath that she would never cross the sea in a plane. "I will see God's face first," she would swear whenever I brought up the subject of us leaving for America. It was not travel my mother feared; it was flight, the lift into the sky.

Crossing the sea was one thing, she told me. After all, you could always jump into the water if the boat was sinking – my mother could not swim – "but what you could do when the plane begin to fall, eh? Tell me that."

She had crossed the sea in a boat to go to Tobago when my uncle Nate and his wife Iris had had a falling out. Nate had hired a band to come from Trinidad to play at a dance in Scarborough. Convinced that the dance would be packed, the band had come on a hope and a prayer that they would get full pay after the fête.

But things began to go wrong. Iris, predicting failure, refused to cook pots of pelau to sell at the dance. She, a born Tobagonian, was fully aware of her people's general hostility to their bigger sister island. My uncle had not been in Tobago long enough to be accepted, and this bringing in of a band was sure to be resented. Tobagonians, Iris argued, would demonstrate their disdain for

Trinidad by staying outside the dancehall, liming, listening to the sound of the music on the fringe. The pots of pelau and souse would spoil; her money would be wasted, and her neighbours would laugh at them for a long time to come.

My uncle was determined to prove her wrong. He plucked the chickens, chopped the pigs' feet for souse, then sent for my mother to season and cook. She packed us up, my sister and brother and a niece my age, and with bunches of fresh chives and thyme from the Maraval market women on Charlotte Street, bags of yellow onions and red tomatoes because "food too dear in Tobago, oui," we boarded the Tobago boat.

We made the crossing on Thursday night, but by the time we docked I was singing, "Oh, what a night, what a night, what a Saturday night/Oh, what a night, what a night, what a Saturday night", that joyous Calypso refrain, in praise of indescribable pleasure.

On the lower deck, the others had insulated themselves from the chill, inside my mother's coverlet. While they dozed, I had found love with a boy who, as we boarded, had smiled at me from the topdeck, his dark eyes willing me to join him.

Huddled together, we watched the full moon tracking us across the silvery water while his fingers played musical cords on my nipples. Flying fish dance in the Bocas during full moon, people say. If they did, I would not have noticed, nor cared, for my whole body was delighting in a symphony of its own as the boy's fingers rubbed my small breasts into exquisite spasms that today, years later, I still recall with gratitude.

Iris was right. Only a few people came to the dance, but the imported musicians declared my mother's food the best they had ever eaten, and so decided not to kill my uncle the following morning when he could not pay them.

One day we found a snake in the roof. The rainy season had just started, and water was coming in through the galvanize over my mother's bed. We had to endure several days of pot and pans placed strategically on the box spring – the coconut fibre mattress having been safely removed to a corner – before my uncle Nate came from Tobago to climb on top of the house with a bucket of tar to seal the holes in the roof that snakes could crawl through, and bite my mother while she was sleeping.

I held the ladder as he climbed up, and just as he shifted a sheet of galvanize to get to the bottom layer with the holes, he saw the snake.

Startled by the noise, it raised its head in preparation to ward off danger. Resting the tin of tar on the roof, Uncle Nate called to me to hand him a broomstick. I dashed into the house, searched frantically, but could not find the broom, so I pulled out the rod that was propping up the clothes line in our backyard.

My mother, hoping to catch the brief respite of morning sun, had just hung three lily-white sheets on the line. They dropped to the muddy ground as I ran with the pole back to my uncle on the ladder.

He had backed down to the lowest rung. He took the pole and poked the snake. It fell. My uncle rushed inside the house and I, right behind him, saw the snake's orange and black body struggling to wind itself through the wire coils of my mother's box spring.

Did I scream? I must have, because my mother's hand, smelling of blue soap, was over my mouth, and her voice was quietly insisting that I shush.

"Don't frighten the poor thing," she was saying. "It's not going to hurt you."

She pushed me gently into Uncle Nate's arms, lifted the box spring, and with the snake coiling and uncoiling, hissing and flicking its forked tongue, she dragged the box spring through the back door, down the back steps, and into the yard. All the while, Uncle Nate was shouting at her, calling her mad, demanding that she leave the snake to him. He reached for a shovel to bash in its head. I wanted him to kill it. Kill it dead.

My mother ignored us. With gentle prods from the pole, she helped the snake get out of the coils and onto the ground.

"Hold the dog," she commanded me, as it tried to rush at the snake. Slowly, with the dog barking, my uncle protesting, and I shivering in fear, my mother nudged the snake until it slithered on its own into the bamboo touffe at the back of the house.

Despite the old Indian woman's assurances that bamboo

brought good luck, I remained afraid that the snake would breed and multiply and one of them would, one day, get my mother.

In time, though, I developed a compelling interest in boys that diverted my attention from my mother's safety.

Years passed. My sister Velma and I went to America. To celebrate Velma's graduation from medical school, I invited my mother to join us in New York. On the long list of reasons that I had prepared in defence of the safety of flying, one was that America had landed a man on the moon. My mother wrote back saying that she would never believe that a human being had set foot on the moon, but she was so proud of her girlchild, she would get on a plane.

On the day she was to arrive, the plane emptied and she did not appear. Back in our Brooklyn apartment, a message awaited us from my cousin Marjorie. It said my mother had refused to go to the airport that day because her horoscope had told her it was not a good time to travel. She would come the following Monday.

She came, and lived for twenty-eight years in New York, and although there was much to be fearful of in that city, we never saw a snake.

Just after her 95th birthday, my mother asked us to return her to Trinidad. She had begun to complain about the cold in New York, but Velma and I suspected she had a different reason. Years before, she had bought her plot in the Anglican cemetery, and had made us promise to lay her body there to rest.

She died peacefully two years later, and my Uncle Nate, himself now an old man, but still vigorous and strong, came from Tobago to help dig her grave. I walked behind her coffin to the corner spot she had chosen, and the nearer I came, the more I could see of the tall touffe of bamboo growing just beyond the point where we would rest her head.

BEHIND GOD'S BACK

The story in the newspaper from home said Leela Rampersad, 40, mother of eight, died in a taxi on its way to the San Fernando General Hospital after having swallowed more than a pint of paraquat. Neighbours said Rampersad had been upset after learning that her daughter Vashti, 16, was pregnant for an unidentified black man. Upon learning of his wife's suicide, and his daughter's pregnancy, Manno Rampersad had chopped Vashti in her head with a cutlass. She was in a critical condition in the hospital.

The newspaper was two weeks old. I was reading it in my house, in a country some ten hours away by airplane from where Vashti lay, her head bandaged in white to keep the pieces together.

They must have had to shave her, I thought, before they could stitch her wounds. The strands of her long, straight, black "Indian" hair must have been thickened with blood. They would have had to cut it with shears first before shaving her scalp clean. And how many nurses did it take to hold her head together while the doctor looped his surgical thread from side to side? How deep were the cuts? Did the doctor gently press some of her brains back in with his gloved right index finger? How much blood did she lose? Even if she lived, would Vashti ever be able to think clearly again? And the baby? Vashti had carried it hidden for nearly seven months. The newspaper had said nothing of its condition. I had to know.

I dialled the overseas operator, got the hospital's number, and was put on hold. I would have to wait to hear if Vashti and her baby were still alive.

Time is a hypnotist walking the Sahara. It blows in the eyes of travellers, forcing us to shut our lids tightly against the grit that blurs the moment. In darkness, we cross the sea, wade inland to the vale that was anything but diamond, and there in a green house in a petit valley, the hypnotist whispers "Open sesame."

This is the house I lived in with my mother and sisters. It sits between two Indian neighbours. Mister Pasha, his wife and four children, all under six, is on our right side in a two-storey house with three flags, one orange, one white, one red, flying from bamboo poles staked in the corner of his flower garden to symbolize his religiosity – and high tigerwire fence to protect his property.

No flags flew in the open yard on our left where Mister Ramoutar, his wife Maman, his two daughters Shaz and Ravella, and an older son, Boysie, fought life in a dilapidated board house that leaned treacherously toward the ravine which separated our property from theirs. From our kitchen window, we looked into their single bedroom, lit by a hurricane lamp which cast gargoyle shadows on the bare walls at night. Mister Ramoutar and Maman's coconut fibre mattress lay on the floor near three smaller foam pallets, which were moved to the front room at night for the children to sleep on. Shaz had told me that her parents were saving all their money for Ravella's dowry; that they were hoping to make a match for her that would bring prestige to the family, and that was why they had to sleep on the floor.

The Ramoutar's kept a cow in their backyard, the main measure of their prosperity. The cow supplied us with milk when I and my sisters were sick. I remember, even now, the silky thickness of that milk Maman would squeeze from the cow's nipples and send to our door minutes after my mother had called out to her that "Jenna still has roasting fever from the fresh cold, oui. Some cow milk will do her good."

My sister Jenna and Ravella, both fifteen, were good friends. They walked from the standpipe together each morning with buckets of water on their heads – tall, graceful, like models on a runway. I often heard them giggling at some secret words passed from one of the Maxwell boys across the street as they strolled together to Miss Dorothy's shop for groceries, or to Miss Bartholomew's Hairdressing School where Ravella was taking a course across the road from Mister Bartholomew's Commercial School where Jenna was learning shorthand and typing.

I and Shaz, closer in age, celebrated our youth by dancing the bellaire on the bridge over our ravine in our home-made chambray panties with red rickrack braiding round each leg, which my mother made us on her Singer sewing machine. We knew full well that the Maxwell boys were often peeping. In the middle of steamy August days when rain thundered out of a lightning sky, we climbed Miss Juanita's mango tree to steal hard green verts, to which we added pepper and vinegar for chow.

During school days, if Mister Ramoutar's old car, which he used as a taxi, was working, Shaz would shout across their yard for my mother to make me and Jenna "hurry up, hurry up, nuh, make haste", and we would ride gloriously together in its torn-up back seat with metal springs jamming temporary tattoos into our thighs, waving at our envious schoolmates walking the long walk in the hot sun to our government school six miles down the main road.

At night, before my mother called us to bed, and well before Mister Ramoutar or Boysie, who was as strict as his father, came home, Shaz, Jenna, and I would play hide and seek with the Maxwell boys behind our house. With only blinking candleflies to guide our search, we groped for each other through bamboo touffes, behind the grugru bef and guava trees, outside and inside our latrine, and among the cane stalks my mother planted each year to remind her, she said, of her childhood days in Anguilla, on the sugar estate, when Indian and Black people lived so nice together.

Ricky, the older of the Maxwell boys, was fifteen. The Maxwell family was rich and could easily have afforded to send Ricky to secondary school, but his father wanted him to learn to be a builder so he could inherit his grandfather's construction business. He was a wizard in mathematics and would have liked to teach calculus, he once told me, but he spent his days pouring cement for the house his father was putting up in their back yard to rent.

There was something soft and gentle about Ricky that caused him to hit his thumb with the hammer more often than he hit the nail he was trying to send through the galvanize on the roof. Often, while Mister Maxwell worked at night at his steam laundry in the city, Ricky, and Kent, his younger brother, would slip into our yard for the games we played in the bush.

The rules of the game were that the hiders could not go beyond the boundaries of my mother's yard, but Ravi, Jenna and Ricky, almost always the hiders, would slip under the bridge if the night was warm and the ravine was dry, or cross the road to the house under construction. Often, Kent, Shaz and I, exhausted from our search, would sit on our back steps to await their return. We imagined them whispering nervously about things we dared not articulate, and visiting places we still hid shyly from each other. We let them be. This was their time. Ours would soon come.

It must have happened on one of those nights when we could see only a quarter of the moon, when we were looking up, searching for shooting stars among the hieroglyphs in the sky. Or maybe it was the night when we, the younger three, made a flambeau and climbed Mister Pasha's tigerwire fence to steal the ripe cashews he denied us by day. And where was Jenna? Why hadn't she stayed with Ricky and Ravella? Maybe it was one of those nights when my sister, always irritatingly conscientious, had had to study extra hard to memorize the slanting abstractions of Pitman's shorthand, and for that had abandoned the game early without telling us.

But even if we had not been distracted, could we have prevented what happened? Wouldn't Ravi and Ricky have found some time, some place to be alone? We had known it was for Ravi that Ricky played "Red Sails on the Sunset. I'm longing for you," so hauntingly on his mouth organ on Sunday nights when Mister Maxwell was home and he couldn't dare leave his yard. And didn't he always give her the best of the sour cherries, the juiciest of the julie mangoes, and the chalk picture of Blue Basin waterfall he had so arduously sketched?

There were other signs: the distress I'd read in my mother's eyes as she had watched them dancing close-close like laglee on a hot iron on the night of Jenna's fifteenth birthday party; or Ma's whispered response, intended only for my visiting Tante Lill's ear, in answer to her soft question about "the Indian girl and Mister Maxwell's son." From that conclave of knowing women my mother's fear vibrated: "That is only trouble, oui girl. Maxwell will never let his boy marry no poor Indian girl, and Ramoutar will make a jail before he see his daughter marry a Negro."

I understood this without fully comprehending why. Hadn't Garlo, who lived down the road from us, been banished from her father's house after she had made a baby for Sylvan? Her father had thrown pitch-oil on her and was about to set her on fire when neighbours intervened. Garlo was exiled from the family even though Sylvan's parents had taken the child to live with them. Sylvan disappeared one night. His chopped up body was found in Brunton's gully two days later and people whispered that his toti was missing. His killer was never caught.

Once a year, on my mother's banister, we lit small wicks in clay pots filled with coconut oil to celebrate Divali in concert with the Ramoutars, who were Hindus. On the night before a million deeya lights twinkled in our valley, Ravella or Shaz would recite again the story of the people of Ayodhya village in India who mourned the exile of their god Rama to a forest, and the kidnapping of his wife Seeta by a demon. "Ram Ram, Seetha Ram. Ram Ram Seetha Ram…" We sang the familiar mantra in chorus as we envisioned this daring godman searching for his love, killing the demon, and being welcomed back to Ayodhya. It was an axiom that Indian men killed to save their women.

A stomach ache kept me home one day. My mother lashed me with her tongue for several minutes for having eaten a whole mamee sipote the night before, then dosed me with a cup of Epsom salts so that I would be reminded, during frequent visits to the latrine, that mamee sipotes should never be eaten after dark. She went off to town, Jenna left for school, and I crawled back under the counterpane, warmed by gulps of bush tea Mammy had forced down my throat. Between sleep and wake I heard my name being called, and moving aside my bedroom curtain, saw Ravi motioning from her backyard for me to open our door to her.

"Why you not in school?" I grumbled, throwing myself back in my bed.

"I went but I come back." She spoke so softly, I barely heard.

She sat on the edge of my bed, her fingers laced in her lap, her head bowed, her long, straight, black hair shielding her face. Her shoulders sagged and she looked as if she were carrying three buckets of rocks around her neck.

"You feeling sick?"

She nodded, and pressed her fingers against her belly. I was about to relate my own misery of mamee sipote and purges but a vague distant look in her eyes that seemed to be gazing on things I could not see, told me she had her own worries and wouldn't be interested in mine.

"I see Miss Phillips leave," she said, referring to my mother.

I pulled myself up on the pillow as I told her that my mother would be gone most of the morning. She listened but I could tell she was drifting in some far-off place. I tried to bring her back: "But something happen to you, Ravi?"

She nodded, her head and shoulders rocking forward and backward, her eyes glazy, like the kid I'd once seen in the orphanage who the nuns said longed for love.

I was beginning to get impatient. As much as I liked Ravi, she was interrupting my rest, and I knew, sick or dying, my mother would be sending me to school the next day.

"I see something last night," she said slowly, her eyes fixed on a spot behind me on the headboard. "I see myself walking barefoot on a pile of hot coals, and all I try to jump off, my feet wouldn't let me. I bawl for Maman and Shaz, for everybody I know to get me off, but the only person who come to save me was you." She caressed the counterpane. "Only you," she said again, and began, gently, to pull the cover off me.

I tugged it back. "What you want from me? You behaving strange, Ravi."

"You think so?" She smiled, but the smile didn't reach her eyes as it usually did. It went inside her, stayed there for a few seconds, and as if it hadn't found a resting place, it came back to her lips and she shook it away and became gloomy again. I drew to the other side of the bed, away from her. She seemed to be in a sort of trance, her body here on the bed with me, her mind travelling in quicksand. She was Ravi, yet she was not. Ravi was a friendly, joky girl. This Ravi was scary, serious. "Lend me the coverlet," she said, and I pushed it towards her with my feet. She folded the cover neatly in two and placed it on the floor.

Then she lay down on top of it, her long skinny legs stretched straight, her thin arms folded above her breast, reminding me of the way Miss Elizer, our opposite neighbour, had looked, laid out in her coffin. "You have to help me." Ravi's voice was clear, quietly demanding, and I, curiosity overwhelming my fear, came off the bed to stare down at her.

"What you want me to do?" Even as I whispered the question I knew I did not want to hear her answer.

"You remember Garlo?" She pulled her lips into her mouth, turned her face to look at the darkness under my bed as if there she would find words to speak the unspeakable.

I nodded. I did not need her voice to describe what I could see.

Her hands, still clasped together, moved down to cover her navel.

"Pa will kill me if he find out," she said. "He warned me plenty times to stay away from Ricky."

I wanted, suddenly, to throw up, to run outside for some fresh air, to put my head under the standpipe and turn the cold water on full blast, but I couldn't move. I stared down at Ravi but I didn't see her face, her arms, nothing but her belly high with Ricky's baby. I closed my eyes tightly but in the darkness behind my lids I saw Ricky's body in the ravine, and Mister Ramoutar's sharp cutlass coming down on his head.

"Oh gawd, Ravi. Your father will kill Ricky."

"I know that," she whispered. "That is why you have to help me."

"What you want me to do?" I cried.

She raised her skirt. She had nothing on underneath. I could see fine black pubic hairs beginning to sprout. "I want you to jump on my belly," she said. "Jump up and down a few times. That will make me lose it."

"I can't do that, Ravi. Please, don't make me do it. It will hurt you."

"I could stand it," she said. "Just do it."

"You could run away," I pleaded. "I'll give you what I have in my penny bank," and I crossed to the dresser, opened my Milo tin and poured my meagre savings onto the bed and began, furiously, to count the coins.

"Twelve dollars," I said. "Here, Ravi take it please. You could have Jenna's too. She has a lot more than me. She wouldn't mind."

"No." She lifted her legs to stop me from crossing to my sister's box. "You have to promise not to tell anybody. Not even Jenna. I dream you saving me. When last you was sick to stay home from school, eh?"

It was true. Except for bloody noses, I was almost never ill.

"You see how things happen?"

"Suppose blood come?"

"Don't worry your head about that. I know what to do. I have something to drink. But hurry up. Time going."

Where could I run? Ravi had dreamed me saving her. My mother had always told us to pay attention to our dreams. When Mister Lezama's young son, Tyrone, had been knocked down on the Main Road by a speeding motorcar, my mother had reminded us that she had foreseen the tragedy in a dream, had warned Mister Lezama, but he had still sent the child down the road to buy cigarettes.

Ravi lay still on the floor, her eyes closed, waiting.

I pulled my nightgown over my knees and up my thighs, made a knot, tucked it into the elastic legs of my panty, and gingerly placed one foot on Ravi's smooth belly. It felt cold; I stepped back.

"Close your eyes," she said without opening hers. "Come on. Try again.'

"No," I said. "I'm not going to do it, Ravi. I can't, I can't." I stood there, transfixed, longing to escape; unable to run out of the room.

"Let me help you." Ravi sat up. She pulled herself nearer to me, drew down her skirt, lifted my right foot, and placed it over her navel. Then she lay back down. "Now raise up you next foot and jump."

Under my bare toes I thought I could feel the slight rise of her navel through the thinness of her cotton skirt, and I tried to put my other foot up but couldn't.

"Help me, please," Ravi begged. "You want Pa to kill me? Eh? You want him to chop up Ricky?"

"I can't, Ravi. Don't ask me, please," and I flung the moist coins onto her body and fled from the room.

Some things I have chosen not to remember; others I will never forget.

I remember Jenna holding me, trying to shush my cries. Mammy had stopped by the Commercial School to tell her to check on me during their recess, and she had caught me running into the yard. I remember Ravi asking Jenna to hand her the stout bottle with the red liquid from her bag to drink. I remember thick blood on my counterpane and on Ravi's thighs and her hem, and I remember her holding her belly and groaning, groaning...

I remember, later, curling up in Mammy's bed while Jenna patted Ravi's head with a washcloth soaked in Limacol, and Ravi whispering to her to say that she had come to our house for help because she had started to bleed.

Neither Mister Ramoutar nor Maman was home, "Thank God," Mammy said, as she sent me to the Main Road for a taxi. Everything would be all right, she said, and resorted to the patois that only she and the older women in the village understood to explain Ravi's condition. (Later, Jenna told me it meant that Ravi's belly had fallen). My mother said she would take Ravi to the hospital; Jenna should go back to school, and I should stay quietly in my bed. "And drink the rest of that bush tea before I come back, oui," she warned.

I tried but could not swallow. My feet were burning, my head was hot, for hours I gripped the pillow to try to keep from shaking as I waited to hear if Ravi and her baby were dead.

"Hello. Hello?" I said into the telephone. "Hello. Anybody there?"

A female voice answered. "You waiting for Doctor Lalroop?"

"Yes," I told her, I'm calling for news about a patient. Vashti Rampersad."

"We don't give news 'bout patients over the telephone," she said rudely. "And too besides, Doctor Lalroop leave the hospital already. He gone 'till tomorrow."

I had not forgotten the respect my people have for titles, so in my most officious English accent, I explained that I was Doctor Pierce, calling from overseas in regard to the health of my niece Vashti, and her baby. What was their condition please?

"Awhaw," her voice, in high octave, expressed a sort of guarded wonder. "You is her relative? In America?"

"Yes," I assured her. "I'm her mother's sister. I'm calling now from my clinic in New York. I do have patients to see, and I've been holding on this line for nearly half an hour."

I could hear her consulting with another female before she came back on the line to tell me that she was sorry to say that Vashti had died that morning.

"What about the baby?" I asked impatiently.

"The baby die too. How that baby could live?"

I buried my head in my hands and cried.

I must have fallen into a heavy sleep because, when I awoke, night had covered our valley and Jenna was placing lighted cocksets about my mother's room, to keep out mosquitoes.

"Mammy come back?" I asked her.

"Yes," she said wearily, and left the room.

Despite the dizziness in my head, I followed her out to the kitchen where my mother sat at the table, her hands propping her chin in sorrow, refusing to drink the bush tea Jenna had brewed for her.

She let me sit in her lap. "The doctor say Ravi has to stay in hospital for a day or so." She rubbed my head. "She lost a lot of blood, but she'll be alright. She's not in trouble any more. Now *you*, Miss Lady, you drink all that bush tea?"

I buried my head in my mother's bosom and cried.

Ravi never went back to Miss Bartholomew's Hairdressing School, and within four months Mister Ramoutar had arranged a marriage for her with an Indian man, much much older than she, from Penal, a village, my mother said, disgustedly, that was behind God's back. But shortly before the wedding was to take place, Ravi left home. Mister Ramoutar never found out that I and Jenna and Ricky had pooled all our savings to buy her a boat ticket to Margarita, an island down the Main, where she could find work in the oilfields. We never saw her again, but one Christmas, two years later, Jenna got a letter from her with two crisp American fifty-dollar bills folded into a flyer announcing RAVELLA'S HAIRDRESSING SALON.

SHANGO

It was the kind of night when all good people stayed inside their homes and children hid under coverlets, afraid of thunder and lightning. Rain fell like pellets from a BB gun, hard and fast to the already soaked earth, and the wind blasted through the trees.

A broken shutter banged loudly against the tapia walls of Pa Azunde's house. Inside its one room, the candle on the nightstand flickered out and its wick drooped into the teacup of soft wax. The old man on the bed rolled over and reached for the box of matches he kept under his pillow. He sat up drowsily and struck a match. It blazed for a second but went out before his trembling hand could reach the wick. He tried three times but each time a gust of wind swept through the room and took the flame away.

"Oba," said the old man, "you up to your old tricks again."

In the darkness, Pa Azunde reached up and pulled the shutter closed and fastened it with a long piece of string attached to the window ledge and looped around a knob on the shutter. Then he struck another match. This time he was able to light the candle. He saved the rest of the flame to light his pipe.

"Might as well smoke," he muttered. "I could see I ain't going to have much sleep tonight."

It was almost dawn. He could hear the cock crowing in Tante Farzie's backyard. Pa Azunde smoked and waited as patiently as he had waited many times before. He listened to the rain and wind duet on the galvanized roof. The two chickens he kept in a wooden box in a corner of the room rustled their feathers and pecked at each other.

"Oba," called the old man, "speak your piece."

Instantly, a bolt of lightning cracked in the room and the blaze of light sent the chickens jumping and clucking in their box. Like

67

a thousand cannons, the thunder broke and the small house quivered.

Pa Azunde puffed on his pipe and listened to the thunder roll away. Then it was quiet; the rain had stopped, the chickens were still, and the wind had died. The candle in the teacup went out again.

"It is a woman," the old man said to the darkness. "A woman with a belly full of trouble, bringing more botheration for my soul."

Tante Farzie's cock crowed four times as Pa Azunde got out of bed to make ready for his visitor.

Elaine sat in the back of the bus holding a handkerchief to her neck. She wondered if the driver had seen the scaly grey spots when she handed him the fare. The ringworm itched and burned her and she kept pressing the handkerchief against it. It was seven in the morning and she was tired. Her buttocks ached from sitting two hours on the wooden bus seat. It would take even longer for them to get to Naparima if the bus, as it threatened, broke down. The driver had been forced to stop once already to check under the bonnet. He had hissed and cussed the Public Transport Company as the rain beat down on his head and shoulders.

Elaine was the only passenger. The driver had looked at her oddly when she boarded and gone straight to the back. She knew that the normal thing to do would be to sit up front and chat with the driver but she wanted to be alone. She wanted to think. She was still not sure that she was doing the right thing.

She leaned against the metal window-frame and whispered some prayers to Saint Francis, her patron saint. The prayers were part of a novena she was making. As she prayed she caressed the blue beads of her rosary, the special one the Archbishop had blessed the last time he had come to her parish.

It was Father Otega, her priest, who had suggested the novena after Elaine had gone to him in tears. She had tried for weeks to pretend that nothing was wrong, not wanting the priest to know her shame, but soon it became too much for her to bear alone. She broke down.

"I can't take it any more, Fader. I just have to tell yuh what Harold doin to me and de children."

"Be calm, my child." Father Otega patted her shoulders. "God is our comfort in times of need and sorrow."

"It look like God turn his back on me, Fader." Elaine sobbed and her shoulders shook.

Harold, her husband, was practically living with Beulah, the biggest whore in the village. At first, Elaine told the priest, Harold was really sly about it. He stayed out a couple of nights every now and then, and she thought he was playing draughts with Mister Critchlow, his friend. But Critchlow had come by the house one evening when Harold was out and told her that he had not seen Harold in weeks. When Harold came in that night she mentioned Critchlow's visit. She asked him, "Who you playin draughts wid now?"

Harold replied, "What make you tink I playing draughts wid anybody else?"

Elaine had not known what to say in reply.

But talk was floating about the village that Harold was spending time with Beulah. The children heard it and told Elaine. Elaine couldn't, wouldn't believe it at first, but it had her worried.

Harold was always so quiet that he was the last man anyone would suspect of doing something like that. She asked him one night if he knew the lies people were saying about him and Beulah.

"People so jealous dey will say anyting to break up a good marriage," she said, watching him closely.

"Is true, Elaine," Harold told her, without looking up from his food. The relief in his voice was that calm after the storm that nobody talked about. "Beulah is meh woman now." He pushed aside the plate of rice and peas she had placed before him, and left the house…

"Oh Gawd, Fader Otega, I can't hold meh head up in public no more," Elaine cried. "De man makin me shame shame in de whole village."

"You must pray, my child," said Father Otega. "You must make novenas and ask the saints and the Virgin Mary to intercede on your behalf. Come, let us light some candles and pray."

For weeks Elaine lit candles – at the church, in the grotto of the Virgin Mary, and at home. On Sundays she went to High Mass and put ten-dollar notes into the collection plate. On Wednesdays she went back to church for early morning service. On Saturdays she went up to Mount Saint Benedict to pray with the monks.

Harold moved all his clothes to Beulah's house.

Elaine's Indian friend, Pourie, told her one day, "Girl, yuh look like yuh have marasme. Yuh lookin tin-tin and yuh hair falling out."

Elaine smiled weakly and continued to hang clothes on the line.

Pourie came over and sat on the back steps of Elaine's house. She folded her hands across her breasts and said, "Elaine, yuh is ah big fool. Yuh mean dat you goin to jus sit down and let dat brazen hussy take yuh husband away?"

Elaine hung the last shirt on the line and sat down besides Pourie.

"I doh know what else to do, Pouri. Father Otega tell me to make novenas. I do all dat. I light candles, I pray, and still the man living wid Beulah. Is true he still does come by on Friday and leave some money for the children, but dat is all."

"Look, why yuh doh go and see somebody about dis ting?"

Elaine pretended not to understand her friend.

"Who somebody you talkin 'bout?"

"Doh play de fool wid me, Elaine," Pourie said. "Yuh know full well dere's people who could fix a ting like dis. How you tink Beulah manage to get she hooks in a good good man like Harold in the fust place? Is obeah dat woman workin left, right and centre. Yuh can't fight obeah like dat wid no candle."

Elaine cupped her lips. "My Gawd, Pourie, doh talk so loud 'bout dat kinda ting around here. I is a good Catholic. I in church two, three times a week. I can't be going to no obeah man."

"Okay," said Pourie. She got up and straightened her skirt. "If you want Beulah to keep Harold, dat's all right wid me. Jus yesterday I see she wid two big new gold bangles on she han'. Dey mus be wurt' over 200 dollars. Harold sure spennin' a bundle on dat woman." And she went back to her house.

For days Elaine pondered her friend's advice. When she went

to High Mass on Sunday she asked God to forgive her for thinking about obeah. She didn't take holy communion that day because she had not gone to confession on Saturday. She didn't want Father Otega to know what she was thinking.

The next morning, Monday, Elaine woke up to find that the ringworm which she had felt developing on her scalp had broken out on her neck. She took one look at it in the bureau mirror and dashed over to Pourie's house.

"Oh meh Gawd," she cried, "de woman put cocobeh on me! Look at meh neck! Oh Gawd, I go dead!"

"Ah hah," Pourie said. "What I did tell you? Dat Beulah ain't makin no joke, nuh. Yuh know how divorce hard to get in Trinidad. She doh want to wait no seven years for Harold. Dat's why she tryin to get you. Yuh have to do someting, girl. Stop playin' stupidie."

"But obeah, Pourie, I never do anyting like dat in meh life."

"Is a fust time for everyting, girl. If yuh doh do someting quick quick yuh ain't goin to have no life to do anyting wid."

Pourie put some flour and water into a pan and began to knead the dough for breakfast roti. She spoke softly. "Leh meh tell you someting. I can't talk too loud because Ramjohn might hear meh." Ramjohn was Pourie's husband.

"Yuh remember last year when me and Ram was fightin' a lot? Every day was blows in dis house. De man used to come home drunk drunk wid no money at all. Every cent he make uses to go in Doolam rumshop. Me and de kiddies almos' starve to death in dem months.

"Well, *papayo*, I decide I wasn't goin take tings lyin down. I went to see de pundit and put meh last ten dollars in he dhoti… A, a, weeks later noting ain't happen. Ramjohn still comin home empty pocket and stinkin drunk. I say to mehself, enough ah dis stupidness. I went to see meh moder in de market. Yuh know she have a fish stall dere. Well, I was feeling so down ah had to cry on she shoulder. An you know what? I had de shock of meh life. Meh moder turn to me and she say: 'Pourie, stop dat damn crying. Here, take dis twenty and stop by de shop and buy a live chicken. Den get on de Naparima bus. I want yuh to go up dere and see a man named Pa Azunde.' She tell me, everybody up dere know 'bout him so jus'

71

ask anybody in de street to show you whey he living. Give him de chicken and de money. I bet Ramjohn stop he arseness.' "

"Well girl, I was never so shock in meh life. Meh moder is a good good Hindu. I never thought she would be believing in no obeah man. I mean, dat's nigger people business, meaning no insult. But I guess times changin in Trinidad and people changing too. Indian marrying Negro, making Dougla children. I tell yuh, de whole world turning topsy-turvy."

"Never mind dat," Elaine said. "What happen wid Ram?"

"What you mean, what happen wid Ram? Yuh does see Ramjohn drunk anymore? Yuh does hear we fighting anymore? I tell yuh whatever dat old man do, he do it well." And she patted out the flour into little balls.

Elaine was still uncomfortable about the whole idea.

"Supposing somebody find out an' tell Father Otega? Yuh know how I always tell yuh he does preach against dat kinda ting. Suppose he find out? Tings like dat doh hide, yuh know."

Pourie said, "Ain't it Fader Otega who always sayin dat de Lord helps dem who help theyself? But is up to you. If I was you dough, I would be on dat Naparima bus bright and early tomorrow mornin."

"Naparima, lady," the driver called back to Elaine. He swung the bus behind the small wooden building that served as the bus depot. The engine moaned tiredly after he turned off the ignition.

Elaine gathered up the two brown paper bags she had stuffed under the seat, hoping that the chicken had not suffocated. Pourie had insisted that she take the chicken and two bottles of sweet oil.

"Is de ting to do," Pourie had assured her.

As Elaine passed the driver he said, "De last bus to Port-of-Spain is t'ree o'clock."

Elaine said "Yes," and almost slipped on the step in her haste to avoid his eyes. The driver grabbed her arm.

"Take it easy," he said. "I does bring ah lot of town people up here. I hear dat man really good. Yuh see dat Indian woman over dere? She could tell you how to get to he house."

"Oh meh Gawd," Elaine moaned silently. "He know where I goin."

72

She hurried over to the old Indian seller as the driver crossed the mud puddles and went into the depot. The woman did not look up as Elaine approached. She kept her eyes on the tray of peanuts, cigarettes, matches and oranges.

"How much is de salt nuts?" Elaine rested her bags between her legs and reached into her purse.

"Is only fresh nuts I does sell, yuh know," the woman said as she continued to peel an orange, her eyes low.

Elaine said, "I never say yuh selling stale nuts. How much is ah bag?"

"Is t'urty cents ah bag."

"T'urty cents! In town yuh could get…"

"Den why yuh doh go back in town an' get what yuh want? I ain't begging." She began to suck the orange, still lookin away from Elaine.

"Is alright, gimme two bags," Elaine told her.

The vendor smiled a little and put down her orange.

"Dey real fresh," she told Elaine. "I does roast dem every night mehself."

Elaine cracked open a nut. "Is true. Dey real fresh." She munched. "You could tell me whey a man name Pa Azunde livin?"

"I doh know no obeah man." The woman bent her head again.

"Dat is jus ole talk," Elaine said. "He's meh uncle. Meh moder only brother. Is ah long time I ain't see him, oui. I livin in Tobago an I doh get over here much."

The woman was silent. Elaine cracked another nut between her fingers.

"I tell yuh what," Elaine said. "Let me have two packs of Anchor. I bet he go like dat." She took two packs of cigarettes from the tray and put down a dollar.

The woman handed her a box of matches. "It free wid two packs." She pointed north. "It ain't far. Is jus dey. It have a galvanize roof."

"What is de house colour?" Elaine asked.

"Is whitewash."

Elaine tucked the nuts and cigarettes into her bag and went into the street

She walked for a long while, passing several whitewashed houses, all of them with thatched roofs. Naked children played under the street standpipes, and cows grazed at the side of the road. The smell of manure was strong. The paved portion of the road ended and she rested for a few minutes.

She muttered, "When dese country people tell you someting jus dey, you better get ready for a long long walk." A little boy in a torn white shirt, his penis dangling between his thighs, came up to her.

"Yuh want some help, lady?"

"I lookin for Pa Azunde house. Yuh could show me where it is?"

"Yuh mean de obeah man? Sure. I does make message for him all de time. I does always buy sweet drink for him at Miss Dorothy shop." He reached for one of the paper bags. "Lewee go."

He trotted ahead of her.

"Careful," Elaine shouted, "Doh break de sweet oil!"

They walked for a while. Elaine stopped again to rub her palm. The string handle of the paper bag had made red marks in her hand.

"What I doin in dis place?" she asked herself. "I shoulda never let Pourie talk me into dis." They had left the houses behind. Elaine followed the boy past gardens of lettuce and tomatoes and across a two-by-four that spanned a dry ravine.

"Is over dere." The boy pointed to a house which stood back from the road, almost hidden by two huge zabocca trees. Elaine took the bag from the child and gave him a shilling and a bag of nuts. He ran back down the road. She took out the rosary from her skirt pocket, wrapped it in her handkerchief, and pushed it far down into her purse. "Holy Mary," she whispered, "moder of God, pray for us sinners, now and at de hour of our death, amen."

She raised her hand to knock on Pa Azunde's door, but before she could knock, a voice called. "The door ain't closed. Come in."

It was the Friday following Elaine's visit to Pa Azunde. She had done exactly as he has ordered: rubbed the sulphur on her neck twice a day, taken a hot bath with the leaves he had given her, and gone to the sea for a swim on Wednesday morning.

She had missed mass on Wednesday and Father Otega had

ridden his bicycle up to her house. "I felt something must have happened. You have never missed the Wednesday morning mass. How you doing, my child?"

Elaine turned to get him a glass of water from the fridge. "I doin okay oui, Fader. I jus had to do someting dis mornin, dat's all."

"It must have been very important to make you miss mass…"

"Yes," Elaine agreed, "is someting ah had to do for Harold."

"Oh, he is back then! But that's wonderful! God be praised!"

Elaine said, "How de collection goin for de parish hall, Fader?"

"Not too bad," he answered. "Things are hard all around but people are trying. The bazaar this weekend should help considerably. We'll see you there, I hope."

"Oh yes," Elaine said. "I go be at High Mass, too."

Father Otega drank the glass of water and said goodbye.

Elaine felt bad for the rest of that day. She thought of going to confession, but Pourie came by the house and said:

"Girl, yuh lookin better already. Yuh see what I did tell yuh. Dat man is Obeah fader!" Elaine forced all thoughts of confession out of her mind.

She felt better on Friday. The ringworm was drying up and her hair didn't fall out in lumps when she combed it. She cooked a big pot of pelau that afternoon. She had seasoned the chicken the night before and the smell of curry filled the house.

Elaine added a piece of chive and turned the boiling rice. She checked her watch. It was almost six. Harold always came by about that time on Fridays. Harold liked curry pelau.

"One ting yuh could say bout dat man," Pourie had told her, "He does never forget to bring dat money on ah Friday."

Elaine had agreed. "No matter what happen between man and wife, a man should always mine his children."

She lowered the flame under the pot and went into the bedroom. She wasn't sure Harold would eat any of the food. She had asked Pa Azunde: "But suppose he doh want to eat de pelau? He doesn't eat home anymore, yuh know. I sure dat woman tell him not to eat anyting from me."

"Doh worry yuh head bout dat," the old man has assured her. "He go eat."

In the bedroom, Elaine checked herself in the bureau mirror.

As she raised her hand to her hair she knocked over the small statue of the Virgin Mary which she had kept on her bureau for years. The head broke and rolled under the bed. Elaine stared down at the piece of white marble. "Oh Gawd," she cried. "Is ah sign, ah bad sign!" She pushed the body under the bed and hurried out of the room.

She wanted to tell Pourie about the statue but remembered seeing her go up to the spring with a basket of clothes.

Elaine sat at the kitchen table and talked to herself.

"Is not bad I doin. God doh punish people for helpin deyself. I jus can't sit down an let dat bad woman get everytng I work so hard for. She doh even know what de inside of ah church look like. I can't jus let she take Harold away. De poor man doh even know what he doin. She have him so basodee."

Smoke was coming from the pot on the stove. Quickly, she turned off the burner and moved the pot

"If I ain't careful, I ain't go have no pelau, only bun-bun." She stirred the food and hummed a Catholic hymn.

"Oh queen of the Holy Rosary, oh bless us as we pray, and offer these our roses, of garlands day by day."

Harold pushed open the back door and came into the kitchen.

"Whey de children?" he asked.

"Dey playin cricket down in de savannah."

Harold sat down at the kitchen table. Elaine said, "Yuh want some ginger beer?"

"Ginger beer does give me too much gas these days," Harold said. "Yuh have any pelau left? I could smell dat curry from way down de road."

"Is jus a little chicken and rice," Elaine said. It ain't have no peas in it. Dem Indians want ah dollar ah pound for dry peas in de market." She dished out a plateful for him.

Harold said, "Man, everytng goin up. I jus hope Eric Williams know what he doin. Even buildin materials gone sky high."

"Well, is all yuh who vote for him," Elaine said. "All yuh want independence. All yuh wasn't happy wid de white people ruling yuh. Negro people always want someting because it stylish. Jus because Jamaica get independence, all yuh want it too. Wait an see how much hell we go ketch."

Harold said, "Tings bound to get better. Is black people in power now."

Elaine took a zabocca from the top of the fridge. She asked Harold, "Yuh want ah piece ah zabocca?"

"Yes, leh me have a little piece dey. Is ah long time I ain't have ah nice piece ah zabocca. Put some hot pepper on it for meh."

Elaine took the bottle of pepper sauce from the back of the cupboard where she had hidden it that morning. She shook the bottle and then poured a spoonful of sauce on to a slice of zabocca. She sat down at the table and watched Harold as he ate.

She felt proud. He had never discussed politics with her before.

Elaine asked him, "You want some more pelau? You know de children doh like it much."

Harold scooped up the remaining grains of rice and pushed the plate toward her. "Yes, leh me have a little bit more. Is a long time I ain't eat a good curry pelau."

While he ate, Elaine went into the living room and brought back two detective novels.

"Velma send dese for you," she told Harold. "She remember how you like to read detective novels."

Harold smiled as he flicked the pages of the books. "Is de furst time any of yuh family give me anyting. Dat moder of yours doh even like meh head."

Elaine said nothing. She knew he was right. The first time her mother had seen Harold she had said, "Dat man looking sly sly. You can't trust dem kinda men at all. You ain't even know de man from Adam, but you talkin 'bout love."

Elaine had replied, "But Mamma, he ain't too long come from Barbados and already he stablish as a contractor. He does draw plans and tings and build house all over Trinidad. Besides, is Sidney who introduce me to him and you like Sidney."

Her mother had exclaimed, "Sidney! Sidney is de biggest fowl tief in Sangre Grande! He was in jail twice for dat. I bet dat's whey he meet Harold. I just don't trust dem quiet, sly people. You never know what dey go do."

Mama was right. Harold was always so quiet you never knew what was going on in his mind. The only things he liked to do was play draughts and read novels. No one would ever have expected him to go and live with a woman like Beulah.

Harold got up from the table and pulled out his wallet. Elaine watched as he counted out some money and placed it on the empty plate.

She said, "But you ain't see de chilren so long. Why yuh doh wait an see dem. Dat cricket match mus be almos over."

Harold thought for a minute. Then he said, "Is true." He picked up the two novels and went toward the gallery.

Elaine smiled. Everything was going just as Pa Azunde had said it would. Pourie was right. That man is obeah fader. Quickly, she rinsed the plate and covered the bottle of pepper sauce. She put the zabocca skin in the rubbish pail, tucked the money in her bra, and went up to the front of the house.

Harold was sitting in his chair in a corner of the gallery, reading. As he read, he rubbed the corns on his toes. Elaine watched him. She felt good all over. She had not seen him in that way for a long time. She told him, "I have to see Pourie about someting. I goin be right back."

Harold didn't respond, but Elaine did not mind. She knew that when Harold found a book he liked he forgot about everything around him. She ran over to Pourie's house.

Pourie said. "I see de man dey dey in he gallery readin book jus like not'ing ain't happen. You mus be put someting in de man food, girl." She laughed loudly.

Elaine said, "Doh say tings like dat 'loud. Bush have ears you know." But she laughed too. "Girl, I never see anyting like this. Everyting dat ole man tell me come true. Is ah miracle."

Pourie told her, "It ain't no miracle. Is just dat Pa Azunde obeah stronger dan Beulah obeah. Talkin bout Beulah, what you tink she go do when she pass and see Harold sittin in de gallery like dat?"

Elaine said, "I doh know, girl. De woman so rotten she could do anyting. I know is wrong, but I wish dat man she was livin wid last year had killed she instead of jus givin she a stab."

Pourie said, "Dem kinda barracuda does live forever. Is good good people like you and me who does dead fust. I hear she went to a Shango de other day."

Elaine was immediately frightened. "Shango! Oh Gawd, whey you hear dat from?"

Pourie told her, "Tallboy was dere. You know how he like dat kinda ting. He tell me Beulah ketch power for so. She was tremblin and rollin all over de groun in dat blood an dirt."

Elaine said, "Yuh tink I better run up to Naparima again?"

"Nah," Pourie assured her. "Pa Azunde could beat back Shango any day. Look how the ting workin already."

"Is true," Elaine agreed. "I go wait and see. I better get back home. Dem chilren comin home soon wid all dat mud from de savannah." She hurried out.

Beulah was trying hard to get a taxi. The Friday afternoon crowd swarmed over the taxi stand, shoving and shouting destinations to the drivers. Few cars were making the run to Diego Martin because heavy rains had flooded the Main Road. Beulah spotted a familiar yellow Rambler coming down Frederick Street. She pushed through the throng, and waved at the driver. The car pulled up alongside the curb. Beulah put her hand on the door handle.

The driver said, "Sorry baby, I ain't goin to Diego today. It takin too long to make dat run. I goin to San Juan."

A man pushed Beulah aside and got into the taxi and it drove off. Beulah shook her fist and shouted, "Is so all you does make style sometime! Tomorrow you go be beggin for meh fare. I go spit on your arse."

It was after six by the time she got a taxi. She was so tired and irritated by then that she slumped down into the back seat and told the driver to take her straight to her door instead of dropping her at the bottom of the street with everyone else.

The driver grumbled that it would take him too long to get back to town but Beulah offered to pay him two dollars extra, and he agreed. She squinched down between the other passengers and dozed off.

About half an hour later, the driver braked sharply and the car stopped in front of her house. Beulah jerked up. "We here already?"

"Come on, lady," the driver said. "It go take me another hour to fight dat traffic and dat water."

Beulah paid him and went into her yard. She heard her dog barking loudly in the back and wondered why Harold had not untied him as he usually did.

She put her bags down on the front steps and went around to the back of the house. The dog's water bowl was dry and he was straining against the chain. She filled the bowl with rainwater from a barrel and untied the chain.

She went back to the front and carried her bags into the house. She remembered that Harold had told her that the electrical inspector was coming to check the wiring in the house he was building. Maybe they went out for a drink afterwards. "Dem inspectors doh do nothing unless yuh bribe dem."

She started to clean the fish she had brought from the market.

About nine-thirty that evening, Beulah's sister, Joan, came by the house. She told Beulah, "I had to come and see for mehself. I t'ought yuh say dat yuh had Harold tie up like a gym boot. It ain't Harold I see jus now sittin in he gallery readin?"

Beulah laughed. "You ain't know what yuh talkin bout, Joanie. Harold never going back to dat miserable woman. Mus' be somebody else yuh see."

Joan said, "How much people yuh know does sit up and scratch dey toes and read detective novels?"

Beulah was quiet. Then she said, "Is true. He ain't come home today at all. De poor dog nearly die from thirst and he cock-up down dere reading novel. I bet dat Elaine put someting on him."

Joan said, "Nah, Elaine would never do dat. She too churchy. She only believe in God."

"Dem kind is de biggest hypocrites," Beulah said. I t'ought everyting was goin so nice. I did show yuh de two nice gold bracelets he buy for me? An last week he open a bank account in meh name an put t'ree hundred dollars in it. He say dat money is a present because I get him a big contractor job. Meh bossman in de club want a big time bungalow in St. Claire so I tell him 'bout Harold. He give Harold de job. Yuh could bet Harold goin make good money from dat."

"De way it look, de money ain't go come to dis house," Joan said. "Seems to me yuh butterin somebody else bread."

"Girl, doh tell me dat, nuh," Beulah said. "It only goin make me damn mad. When I start frien'in wid Harold it was like blight was on him. He wasn't gettin any big jobs to build house or anyting. So I tell him not to worry, I go fix up tings for him. Dat Elaine better say praise God I get dat job for him, oderwise she would be back cleanin de white chilren bamsee."

Joan said, "Doh get yuhself so hot up, girl. Money ain't everyting. Besides, yuh young an pretty. Dere's plenty more fish in de sea."

Beulah said, "Is not de moncy so much. Is de principle of de ting. Who I look like? Some dog shit for Harold to walk on? Not me. Eh, eh! I tired helpin dese men on dey feet and den havin dem walk out on me. Who dey take meh for? Some bobolee? I ain't lettin no man take advantage of meh again an get away wid it,"

"But Harold ain't take advantage of yuh," Joan said. "If I did know yuh would get so hot up I woulda never tell yuh I see him sittin in the gallery. Maybe de man jus visitin his chilren."

"Dem chilren is jus like dey moder. Dey doh have no respect for Harold. All dey want is he money. Harold tell me dey not nice at all," Beulah said.

"But dey still his chilren."

"I know dat," Beulah snapped. "All de while Elaine tellin people I bad, I never tell Harold to stop givin she money for dem nasty boys. Yuh know, de more I tink about dis ting de more vex I gettin." She slammed a cover on the pot of fish she was cooking and stalked into the bedroom. Joan followed her.

"Doh do not'in foolish," Joan cautioned.

"Sittin here not doin anyting *is* foolish," Beulah said. "Tonight dey havin a big Shango down in de village. I goin down dere. Yuh go see bacchanal in dis place. Harold playin wid me? He doh know who I is!"

She pushed her hair up under a red scarf and patted her face with white powder.

"But what about de cod fish on de stove?" Joan asked.

"Yuh could eat de damn fish," Beulah told her. "Doh let no bone stick in yuh throat."

Beulah changed her dress. She slipped on a white one with big red flowers around the hemline. She took her purse and hurried out of the house. When she came to Elaine's house Harold was still sitting in the gallery, reading. Beulah shouted at him from the street, "You Bajan sucker! You tink you go take advantage of me? A poor woman like me? Not so sucker! We go see bout dat! We go see!"

Harold looked up at the sound of Beulah's voice. He stared at her, then shook his head and went back to his novel. Beulah hurried down the road, her big hips swaying in anger.

Elaine, who had heard the noise and come to the front of the house, went over to tell Pourie about Beulah's threat.

At twelve o'clock, Elaine left her bed and went to check on Harold in the gallery. She asked him, "You ain't comin to sleep?" Harold waved her away and continued to read. Elaine put a glass of ginger beer down on the table in front of him and went back to bed.

Outside an owl began to hoot, and soon another one answered, then a third. Elaine thought, "Dem jumbiebirds really callin tonight."

The hooting continued and Elaine put a pillow over her head to drown out the chilling sound. She fell asleep.

Elaine woke up at six the following morning. Harold had not gotten into the bed so she thought he must have fallen asleep in the gallery. She went out to him. Harold was still sitting in the chair but the book had slipped to the floor and his glasses had dropped to his lips.

Elaine said, "Harold, is six o'clock. Yuh ain't play yuh like to read, nuh." She shook his shoulder and his glasses fell to the floor and broke.

Elaine bent to pick up the pieces of glass. As she came back up, her face came close to Harold's and she realized that his eyes were half open. She touched his cheek. She screamed.

Pourie heard the scream and stopped milking her cow. She ran to Elaine's house.

"He dead! He dead! Meh husband dead! Oh Gawd, I kill de man!" Elaine was screaming.

Pourie pulled her into the kitchen. She said, "Yuh better control yuhself, girl. Yuh ain't kill nobody."

One of Elaine's sons appeared, and Pourie told him, "Run and tell Ramjohn to jump in he taxi and get de constable. Someting happen to yuh father."

The police and an ambulance came and took Harold's body away. "It look like a heart attack," the doctor said, and signed the death certificate.

Pourie warned Elaine not to talk any foolishness about how she had killed Harold; then she went to find some flowers to make a wreath.

Father Otega came. Elaine broke down again and told him about Pa Azunde. She and Father Otega knelt and prayed together for the forgiveness of her soul.

Beulah took sixty dollars out of the bank account Harold had opened for her. She bought a black dress and a new hat with a silver pin on top. She attended the funeral, walking alone, her head held high.

Later that year Lord Moranda, the calypso king, composed a tune about the affair. It went like this:

> Elaine and Harry always in misery
> Elaine say Harold strayin away from she
> So she went to Naparima to see an obeah man
> And she tell him to do whatever he can
> To make Harry come home
> And see he doesn't roam
> Into a next woman's arms.
> But what Elaine didn't know
> Was the woman work shango.
> Shango stronger dan obeah any day
> So the upshot was Harry is dead today.
>
> Chorus:
> Now Harry dead, he dead, he dead
> Is Shango what kill the poor man dead.

On Carnival day everyone sang the song and Lord Moranda won the prize for the best road march.

WATER WOMEN

It was the dry season. Indian children wore sapats to keep hot pitch from oozing between their toes, and the stream in the ravine had long been seduced by the gravel in its bed. Dried coconuts fell from baked branches onto the brittle earth at night, and sand flies and chiggers kept the children in the village hopping. There were few customers in the market and those who strolled through eyed the half-rotten fruits and vegetables suspiciously. Everything was scarce, but nothing was as scarce as water. The standpipes in the streets gaggled and croaked around three or four in the morning and yielded about half a barrel of orange grime. The villagers were at the mercy or the Water Department which sent a truck with two tanks of water once a day to the village.

Two men worked the truck – the driver, an Indian, the helper, a Negro. It paid to know these men. For love or money they would park the truck in front of a house and allow the woman who lived there to run her water hose from the tank to her barrels. Neighbours cussed, and threatened to report the men to the Water Board but secretly they all wished that they, too, could afford to pay the water truck men. But most could not, so they lined up at the other tank with cans, buckets, calabashes, and bowls – anything that could hold water. Families with many children were luckier, for each child, no matter how small, could carry some water. Sometimes the water ran out and the villagers, left waiting with hot empty tins, flung curses at the giggling water truck men, and swore they would never again vote for a blasted government that could send ambassadors all over the world, but couldn't send enough water to the village.

The water truck men were used to such abuse. They revelled in it. It was testimony to their importance. And always, as the

84

truck swayed round the bend in the road, the helper would shout to the children running after it with clanging buckets, "Doh worry. We making another rounds up here later." The promise would pass from neighbour to neighbour, and long into the evening, as the sun hovered just above the hill, reluctant to give the villagers respite from its fury, hopeful eyes would search beyond the bend in the road for the water truck's return.

Jestina was luckier than any of the villagers. She was the water woman for the road gang, and because her house was midway between the stretch of road the government had decided to pave, the water barrels for the road crew were left in her yard. When the water truck came, the men parked in front of Jestina's yard and filled every barrel in sight – the ones that were clearly marked "Water Board Property" in yellow paint, and the two red ones close to Jestina's kitchen door. Unlike Melda who lived next door, Jestina didn't have to pay the men. They had strict orders to fill her barrels – orders that had come straight from their boss, a friend of the foreman of the road gang, for Jestina was more than a water woman.

She had won the water woman's job over some stiff competition. As soon as the villagers found out that the road was to be paved, dozens of them, men and women, had crowded the County Council's office on the morning the gang was to be picked. Some of them knew they were sure to get jobs because they had "buss their tails" getting votes for the party in the last election and somebody better remember that because "election time bound to come round again, just like Christmas."

Only a few positions were open to women. Three or four were needed to pull weeds, and one to tote water for the men to drink. It was common knowledge that the biggest qualification for the water woman's position was what a fella could see in her coming, in her going, and in her bending down.

Nowhere was it written that her breasts had to be as big as Ramjohn's hops bread or that her buttocks needed to be so large that the men would say a thousand times, "Oh boy! That must be jelly cause jam don't shake like that." Such things were understood, and the water woman had to be able to take the picong. These qualities were essential, for they would provide the labourers with some amusement to release the tension of having to dig dirt and rocks and mix cement in the burning sun.

For a woman without such attributes to be hired, she would have to be someone the foreman knew personally – a relative, a friend of a friend, or the wife of a man to whom the foreman owed some favour. Those women in the village who knew they would not qualify in such categories didn't even bother to leave their homes that morning. Except Jestina.

She didn't fit any of the categories. She was short, stumpy, and meagre. She had such small breasts that she frequently stuffed cotton in her bras to fill out the cups. Her buttocks were tight and neat, not too big and not too small. Her complexion was a smooth brown, and she prided herself on never having to worry about "heats" on her face. She did not know the foreman, and she wasn't familiar with anybody influential in the district. But she had one advantage over all the other women: she was a Grenadian. So was the foreman. She got that fact from Roy, the man from whom she was renting, so on the morning when all those people went down to the County Council's office, Jestina went down too.

Suck-finger children who came with their mothers occupied the few half-broken chairs in the waiting room. Jestina waited off to one side of the room. She knew some of the women, but except for a slight tilt of her head to indicate recognition, she spoke to none of them. She saw Melda, her next door neighbour, come into the office and tell a little boy who was sitting on a chair to get off and give her the seat. The child slid off, his finger still in the grip of his teeth. Heaving a big sigh, Melda sat down. She was a big woman, tall and strapping. Children in the village called her elephant woman behind her back. Everything about her was twice the normal size except her head. Her head was very small. It seemed to rest precariously on top her long fat neck.

Jestina watched as Melda took out a big piece of red cloth from her purse and began to fan herself with it. There were only two windows in the room and the dust-laden fan in the ceiling just barely managed to turn.

By midmorning the foreman had picked most of the labourers. By then, children had begun to whimper and cry, hungry and thirsty as they were, many of them dragged to the office with only a little bush tea in their stomachs. The one toilet in the place stank from the odour of urine on the floor splashed by children who had only just made it in time.

Above the noise the foreman shouted a few times for the women to take the children outside, but no one listened. Did he think they were stupid enough to do that and lose their place in the crowd and have somebody else get the job? The man who sat alongside the foreman at the table leaned over and whispered something in the foreman's ear. The foreman nodded and stood up. He raised his hands to get their attention. He said, "To ease up the situation a little, what we going to do now is stop taking labourers, and fill the water woman's job. We go come back to the men after, but these children keeping too much noise and things go move faster once these women take them home. So all all-you woman come up now."

The men moved hastily to one side of the room as the women pushed each other to get to the table. The foreman shouted, "If all you aint stop pushin and shovin, I takin meh book and leave." So they quietly edged each other with their elbows, and sent each other cut eyes.

Melda was in front, the second to reach the foreman's table. The foreman looked up, way up at her. He looked down, shaking his head, wrote her name in his copybook and asked her to wait on the other side. His gaze followed her movement across the room, and it was only after she had finally reached the wall and leaned heavily against it, that he turned back to the next woman in line.

Jestina stood calmly, waiting her turn, and when it came she went up and gave her name to the foreman. While he wrote, she stared at him. When he looked up, she said, "You look jus like some people I know in Grenada. Your face cut off dem."

The foreman's jaws twitched and he squinted at Jestina. He saw her bright brown eyes dancing with the hint of laughter that travelled down to her slightly parted lips. His eyes moved deliberately to her throat and wide shoulders, down to her strong arms that told their own tale of having carried more than their share of heavy load, and his gaze didn't stop there, although it did pause. It went on down her chest, passed her waist, and it was as if he could see through her flowered skirt to her thighs, leathered from years of climbing hills with crocus bags of ground provisions.

His gaze returned to her face. He asked her, "What part of Grenada you from?"

"St. George," she said.

The foreman burst out laughing. "Who you tink you fooling, gurl? I know country woman when I see dem. Turn round dey, let me see your calves." And he came out from behind the table to turn her around as if he was spinning a top. Jestina laughed. She lifted her skirt a little higher so he could see her calves. The women in the line behind her sucked their teeth in disgust.

"Dem calves big like moco yams," he said. "Town gurl doh have calves like dat." He laughed again as he pinched her hip. She jerked forward, bumping her knee against the table. The knee hurt but she kept on smiling.

"Don't handle the merchandise if you ain't buying," she told him boldly.

The foreman took up his copybook.

"Where you living now, Miss Saint George?"

"Buxton Road, right where all you going to pitch," she said.

"All right, Jestina Alleyne, you is the water woman," he said. He closed his copybook, gave it to the man sitting next to him, stood on tiptoe, and announced, "De water woman job full. All you women could go home now."

Well, who tell him to say that. Bacchanal break out. A tall stringy-looking woman with two gold teeth and silver bracelets weighing down her arms sided up to the foreman and with both hands on her hips and amazement in her voice said, "A a, well look my crosses. Since foreday morning I here. All I have in my stomach is a lil' bush tea, and after all dis time you come telling me you giving dis small island woman de work. A, a, buh what kinda arsehole ting dis is at all?"

Janie, in red pedal pushers, a low-back blouse and purple lipstick, shouted, "You ain't know is so all dem small island is?"

And Princetta came from way in back of the room to stand beside Jestina and look her up and down. "What I want to know," she said, "is whey she have dat I have ten times more and plus." She twirled to display her calves.

The foreman steupsed. He said, "I doh want no bacchanal in here dis morning, nuh. Is only one water woman job I had, and I say it full."

"You full of shit, dat's what," a woman shouted. And another one added. "You is ah stinking Grenadian. All you does come down here to we own country and take whey food from we mouth. Why she mus get de job? I could tote water better dan she. I use to tote water all over Maraval. But no, is because she is ah Grenadian too. Is so all you people does be."

And yet another voice broke in, "Eric should send dem all back. Dem tiefing Grenadians, dem stinkin Vincelonians. All dem Bajans. Send dem back!"

They heard her before they saw her. Melda had flown across the room and her fingers were around the front of the dress of the woman who had made the last remark. Melda said, "Who you tink you callin stink? I from St. Vincent and you smell any stink on me? You want see I box out your rotten teeth?"

The foreman sprang on top the table shouting, "I doh want no fight in here! I doh want no fight in here!" And the children danced around Melda and the woman with gleeful shouts of "Heve, heve!"

Melda shook the woman two, three times.

The foreman shouted, "If all you woman know what good for all you tail, you better leave here fast fast before I call police."

The men, who had stood aside enjoying the show, began to shout at the women to go before the police came and shut down the whole place. The women gathered up their children and began to leave, still abusing the foreman, and calling back to their boyfriends and husbands that they shouldn't waste their time because it looked like only Grenadians getting jobs.

Jestina waited with the men. When the last woman had flung her backside in the air and the office door slammed shut, she asked the foreman, "When the job starting?"

The foreman jumped down from the table and wiped his forehead with the back of his hand. "It starting next week Monday," he said a little wearily. "We go have to find a place to put the water barrels."

"I doh see why you can't put dem in my yard," she said. "I doh think the landlord go mind. And too besides, the house is 'bout half way between where all you going to pitch."

"Dat sound good," the foreman said. "Find out from your landlord and let me know by Friday. Den I go have de boys drop off the drums."

"How much dis job paying?" Jestina asked, as if it were an afterthought.

"Thirty dollars a week," the foreman answered.

Jestina's heart jumped. That was much more than she was making doing domestic work. She calculated swiftly. With thirty dollars she could now throw two susu hands instead of one, and reach her goal twice as fast. She looked at the foreman. "You must be skylarking, man," she said. "You expect me to tote water in de hot hot sun for a measly thirty dollars? Slavery ent dead?"

The foreman looked at her, amused at her boldness. "I tell you what," he said. "Wait till I finish up here. Maybe you could make someting on de side." The men all burst out laughing, and Jestina joined them.

"You tink you could handle dis?" she asked the foreman, and patting her behind, she shook her way to the door. There she turned and waved to the laughing men. "I go see all you next week." The men waved. They liked her. She could parry. She would make a good water woman.

THE GREEN CARD

Loris wanted to go home bad. For weeks, that was all she had been talking about to her friend Selena. This day was no different. From the minute Selena had come through the back door, Loris had started moaning about home, home.

"Is a funny thing, you know," she said, "I in America eight long years. I never feel homesick. Not one day as God send I ever wake up wishing I was back home. I meet Carl, and what happen? Bap! I want to go home bad bad."

"I warn you more than once about that man," Selena reminded her. "From the time I set eyes on him, I could see he is a sagaboy. Every word come out his mouth have to do with fête, carnival or Trinidad. He's behaving like a real never see, come see. What's wrong with that man?"

"He's a real Trini, girl," Loris smiled. "And with carnival coming, all he talking about is home, home. Every time the man call me he talking about going down for carnival. He bring back a whole batch of memories."

"Well, girl," Selena declared, "you could go back if you want, but I never want to see that backwater place again. You can't pay me to go back there."

"You see how the Yankee dollars does make you West Indians turn your back on your motherland?" Loris laughed. "Not me, girl. I not selling my heritage for nothing. Not even a green card."

"I could go back home if I want to," Selena said. "*I* get my green card long time. But what I going back down there for?"

"*You* have a green card?"

Loris's tone stung Selena, and she responded angrily. "What you mean asking a question like that? My madam sponsor me since 1972."

"Your madam sponsor you?" Loris laughed. "What madam sponsor you? Girl why you like to lie so, eh? You don't have to lie to me. I not going to report you to the immigration. You is my homegirl."

Selena wanted to insist that she *did* have the green card. She wanted to convince Loris that she was one of the lucky ones who didn't have to panic every time they saw strange men coming up the madam's driveway. The ones who didn't live in constant fear of being caught, put on a plane, and sent back home with only the clothes on their backs. She wanted so much to be able to prove that she was a permanent resident, but she knew if she kept insisting that she was, Loris would challenge her to produce the green card. Instead, she got up from Mrs. Ames's (Loris's madam) kitchen chair, picked up the big silver handbag she had purchased in Macy's basement for $3.95, and said she had better go to the bus stop and wait for Sally Ann "before the white lady's child have to walk home by herself and some man come by and snatch her, and I get my arse in trouble."

"Then you'll really have to run back home in true." Loris laughed as Selena hurried out. But she didn't laugh long. Who was she to laugh at Selena, anyway. Her position was no better. She couldn't go home either.

That evening, as she prepared the Ames's dinner and during the long two hours she spent cleaning up the kitchen, wiping out the oven with a Brillo pad, scrubbing the burners, mopping the floor with bleach, getting down on her knees to wipe up the sticky jelly stains that the Ames's children had dropped under the kitchen table, then taking the trash out to the large bin by the garden shed, Loris thought about home, about mas' in the Savannah, fête down Wrightson Road, going down Saint James for a roti, oh God!

Later that night Carl called her from Brooklyn where he lived with his brother, Knolly, to tell her with incredible joy that he had booked his passage. "I flying Pan Am, girl. Ticket cost me $700, round trip."

"But why you buy such a dear ticket?" Loris had half-hoped he would say he had bought one for her too, not because she knew she could go, but because it would show how much Carl liked her. She tried to keep the disappointment out of her voice as she said, "I hear you could get excursion fare for $395."

"You think I want to get stuck down there?" Carl told her. "Excursion fare is only bacchanal, oui. Knolly went down by excursion fare last year, and you know what happen? He couldn't get on a flight to come back for four days! They overbook! Knolly almost lose his job. I had to call and tell his bossman that Mama dead, and Knolly have to stay for the funeral. Not me, girl. Is a lot of smart men who running excursions from New York. You pay your money, have ticket in your hand, but when you get to the airport, they tell you the plane full up. I have my work to come back to, *papayo*. I can't risk no excursion thing."

"So when you leaving?" Loris asked, still hoping that the question would offer him an opening to say something about her accompanying him. But Carl was a man who would stump his toe on a big stone right in front of his eyes. He didn't take the bait. Instead, he went on to boast about how he was leaving on the Friday before Carnival in time to catch Panorama, Dimanche Gras, and to jump up Jour Ouvert morning with San Juan All Stars. He said he wanted her to go but he obviously had no intention of paying her fare. This realization was like a stab in her heart from a sharp icepick, so Loris consoled herself that she couldn't go anyway. Yet, with each mention of a fête that she would miss, of a steelband she wouldn't hear, of mas' she wouldn't see, her temperature rose, her blood boiled, her head ached, until finally, she couldn't stand the tension anymore, and she told Carl that she had to hang up because Madam was calling her.

She wished she had never met Carl. She was okay before she met him. It wasn't that she had never thought about going home. She had often thought about it, but she had never *longed* for it. She hadn't heard before, as she had been doing for weeks, the sounds of Desperadoes steelband playing "Ting Tang Darling" in her ears; she hadn't seen, flashing before her eyes, blinding her with colour, Beryl McBurnie's dancers doing the bellaire on stage at the Queens Park Savannah; and it was a long time since she had remembered, with pleasure and a little embarrassment, the way she shook her bottom down Frederick Street behind Solo

Harmonites, rubbing up against Mervyn, her old boyfriend, drinking rum in the town, and how her picture had appeared on Ash Wednesday morning in *The Guardian* above a caption that said: "Trini Women Get On Bad For Carnival". Oh God, she didn't want to remember! But Carl was bringing everything back, and she was getting withdrawal pains. She should have known not to get involved with him.

When she had met him at a West Indian house party in the Bronx, the first question she had asked him was whether he went home for Carnival. That was what she called her "sizing up" question. If a Trini man said he usually went home for Carnival, she knew right away to start looking in another direction. But even after Carl had laughed and boasted that he had missed only two Carnivals in the twelve years he had been in the States, something kept her from walking away. Maybe it was his shoulders. He had wide, strong-looking shoulders, and she liked men with shoulders like that. On top of that, Carl was short and dark, two features that she fell for in men. "The blacker the berry, the sweeter the taste," she would tell Selena when her friend wondered why she liked dark-skinned men.

"I believe in lightening the coffee, girl," Selena said. "And besides, you so tall. Why you like them short, short-arse men?"

"I figure like this," Loris had explained patiently, "If a short man want to take me out, it must mean he doesn't have a short man complex."

"But when you dancing, you can't even rest your head on his shoulder. And you can't wear high heels when you go out with a short man," Selena complained. She considered herself a first-class dresser, and first-class meant wearing high, high spiked heels, even if she had to inch her way across a room looking like Marilyn Monroe on a tightrope. High heels were especially hard on her feet after a tough week's work in Mrs. Duant's kitchen in New Rochelle but she wore them anyway.

"Carl doesn't mind if I wear high or low heels, girl," Loris had assured Selena after she had been out with him a few times. "My height doesn't bother him at all. He's a man of stature."

Carl was indeed different from the few men she had gone out with in America. He didn't drink and he didn't smoke. And he liked to dance, a factor that made him even more appealing. And on top of that, the first time he had come up to New Rochelle to see her, he had brought her mangoes. Never mind that they were forced-ripe, and uneatable. They were mangoes, a little bit of home in America, and no man had been so thoughtful, so aware of her homesickness before. Certainly not Thomas, the Black American from Alabama she had married.

The marriage was not something she liked to think about, but it came rushing to the surface of her mind as she thought about Carl and home and Carnival and how much she longed to bathe in the sea down Carenage, to taste the salt water, to feel it washing off the blight. She felt a longing to go for a walk in the Botanical Gardens to see the lily ponds. She and Mervyn used to sit on the rocks near the lily ponds and talk about how they would go to New York together. That didn't work out. All the while she and Mervyn had been making plans, he was seeing Thelma, her best friend, behind her back. She should have known better than to get involved with Mervyn. When she heard the report, Thelma was pregnant. And brass-face Mervyn had had the gall to ask her not to leave him. She *had* left. She left the following month for America alone, and before she was six months in the Yankee man's country, she had met and married Thomas.

She didn't love Thomas. She had married him so that she could stay in America. Plain and simple. Thomas, a janitor at the YMCA on 135th Street, just down the way from the apartment building she lived in back then, had expressed his appreciation of her body several times as she had passed by the "Y" to and from the subway. Alone in New York, in the height of the summer of '68, with heat rising all over the country, Loris had seen, in Thomas's interest, opportunity for a little romance and, more importantly, an extension of her holiday visa, a legalization of her status.

She accepted his invitation to come up to his apartment to look at his TV. When she got there she was not surprised to find that not only did Thomas not have a TV, he didn't even have a radio. His "apartment" was a two by four room that was a sweatbox in summer and a freezer in fall. In winter, the landlady put on so little heat that Thomas had to sleep in the men's locker room at the YMCA.

Loris didn't embarrass him about the TV or the room. She sat on the bed – he didn't have a chair – and they spent that first date talking, eating barbecue ribs and white bread that Thomas had run out to get from the rib joint on 125th Street, and sipping gin. Early the next morning, before she went to the communal bathroom down the hall to sponge off, she confessed to Thomas that she really liked him, yes. And Thomas, not too long out of Tuscaloosa, forty-two years old – a countryboy, he called himself – with little experience in fondling anything but old Chevy engines, seemed in awe of this nice woman with a pretty accent who had come all the way from a land that he had never heard of before, an island surrounded by water, but who, he was amazed to hear, didn't know how to swim. He said he wanted to teach her.

They got married two months later. She had insisted that the marriage took place in a church, so one Saturday morning she and Thomas took a taxi over to the Anglican church near Central Park. It was raining that morning and she thought the rain might be showers of blessings, but later, after Thomas did what he did, she realized that the water was a bad sign. Manzy, the taxi driver, had to be their witness because Thomas's friend, who had promised to stand up for them, was too drunk to make it. As it was, Thomas himself could barely put on his shirt and tie, and that was a bad sign too. She should have known better than to marry him. He couldn't even swim.

The man seemed to stay drunk. Why hadn't she noticed that in him before? Maybe she had. Maybe that was one of the reasons she had thought her plan would work: Marry him, get him to sign the papers, get fixed up, then disappear before he could open one eye. Later, she would file for divorce. But life doesn't always work out the way you want it.

Thomas lost his job at the YMCA after repeated warnings about excess chlorine in the pool and too much soap on the tiled floors. After that, Loris had to take care of him because he couldn't stay sober long enough to get another job. He came constantly to her work – she had taken a sleep-in job in New Rochelle – to get money, and when she didn't have it to give him, he would get abusive.

When she asked him, on a visit to his room three months later, to go with her to an immigration lawyer to sign some papers because her holiday visa was about to expire, he refused.

"I know about you West Indians," he told her. "You want to marry American men so you can stay in this country. Mah friend told me about you all. But you gonna have to pay for this, baby."

She realized then that it was time to make the best of a bad situation. "How much you want?" Disgust slipped like slime off her tongue. Thomas did not seem to notice.

He was in his element. "How 'bout some pussy?" he laughed. "You ain't give me hardly any since we been married. Come on, sugar. Give your old man a piece."

She backed away, revolted by the stench of his whisky breath. Jesus, she thought, the things this country does make you do!

His anger flared. "Bitch!" he spat. "I ain't signing no fucking papers unless you give me some pussy. You West Indian girls think you too good. Mah buddy warned me about you. He said you only wanted marriage to get your papers fixed. You…" He raised his hand to slap her but she ducked. He tried again, but she stayed him by unbuttoning her blouse quickly. His anger began to cool as she reached into her bra. He pulled her down on the bed, but she smiled for him to wait. Instead of her breasts, she pulled out a twenty dollar note and dangled it in front of his eyes.

She tried to be sweet. "Why don't you go buy us a bottle? I feel like having a drink."

He wasn't immediately taken in. She had to caress his cheek and allow him to put a hickey on her neck before he would take the money. As soon as he was out of sight, she grabbed her bag and fled from Harlem.

Her agency got her another sleep-in position in New Rochelle. She paid a lawyer in Chinatown $500 to file the papers for her without Thomas' signature, but she never heard a word from the immigration people. The lawyer kept telling her that these things took a long time.

A year went by, then two. She waited, hiding out, moving from one sleep-in job to another. She wrote home and sent money, but never knew if they had received it because she was too afraid to put her return address on the letter. She had heard that that was one way immigration traced illegal aliens. She kept trying to call the lawyer, until an operator told her the number was disconnected.

Then one Saturday, just before Christmas, she was on the IRT on her way to Nostrand Avenue in Brooklyn to buy some mauby bark and a few packs of dried sorrel when she saw him. Thomas. He was hanging onto a strap at the other end of the subway car and she, scanning the area for a vacant seat, met his eyes. As she stared, wanting to turn away and yet not being able to, she saw recognition spread across his face. He lurched toward her in surprise, calling out her name. The train braked to a stop and she rushed out. He followed her up the steps, calling her name, shouting to people that she was his wife, that he hadn't seen her in a thousand years. Loris wanted to die.

He came after her, up into the street, onto Eastern Parkway. Looking around frantically, she saw that she was on Church Street, miles from Nostrand Avenue. What should she do? She kept on going, hoping that he would falter, that he would be too drunk, as usual, to keep up. But it was she who faltered. She slipped on the icy pavement and fell, hitting the back of her head. By the time she had managed to get up and get to a bench on Eastern Parkway, he had caught up to her.

"What you want?" she demanded, the angry words spewing out as she grimaced from the pain in her right ankle and her head.

"I want mah baby," he said, breathing down on her. "You mah pretty West Indian baby." He reached out to touch her, and she slapped his hand away.

She was cold and angry. "Drop dead, Thomas! Just go hide yourself in a hole and leave me alone."

He moved closer to her, his body shivering, his teeth chattering, words sputtering out on his dry icy breath. "I... I been looking for you, babe. I looked all over. Even... even went up to New Rochelle. Why you treat me so bad?"

She looked at him, then stared at him as if she were seeing him for the first time, as if she was trying to fathom the insanity that had led her to marry him. Suddenly she laughed. A sad, crying sort of laugh. A laugh at herself. At the lies she had written home about her American husband. She would have to write one day and tell them he was dead.

Thomas shook his head, not comprehending her mood. He reached up again and touched his icy fingers to her cheek, and something, something in that pathetic gesture, touched the rock in Loris's heart.

"Why you out in this freezing weather without gloves?"

"I don't need no gloves." He rubbed his hands together. "I got you, babe. You mah baby. Why you run out on me?"

A strong wind ripped by and Thomas pulled his jacket about him and Loris noticed its thinness.

"Can't you buy a decent winter coat?"

He shook his head. "What makes you think I don't got one? I could show you plenty coats. I even got me a leather jacket."

"Sure," Loris nodded. "And you got a television, and a…" She winced as a sharp pain tore through her ankle. "God," she moaned, "I need an aspirin."

He pointed to a drugstore at the corner. "We can get some over there. Want me to go get it for you?" She nodded and he got up, but he hadn't taken two steps before he looked back. "You not gonna run away again, are you?"

Loris tried to smile. He came back. "Why don't we both go? Then you can get a cup of coffee to swallow the pill with." He stretched out his hand. Loris hesitated but the pain in her foot was getting worse, and the wind was picking up. How long could she stay on a cold bench on Eastern Parkway? She held his arm and hobbled over to a booth in the back of the drugstore.

He ordered two coffees and a small paper pack of painkillers and she swallowed three. Slowly, as the minutes passed, the pain in her ankle receded and her head, too, began to feel better. Thomas, braced by two more cups of coffee, and a pack of cigarettes that Loris paid for, told her he was living in Bedford Stuyvesant. She wrote the address on a napkin, while he begged for hers.

She lied. "I living in Brooklyn too," she said. "I staying with a friend. You know how some people funny. She mighten like me giving out her address. Anyway, I moving out early in the new year. I could give you the telephone number, though." She wrote the number of a West Indian record shop in Brooklyn on another napkin, and Thomas folded it carefully and placed it in his jacket pocket. Then, probably because she felt a little guilty, probably because it was Christmas – she wasn't sure why – Loris bought him a pair of cheap gloves and a scarf from the drugstore, and gave him ten dollars. An hour or so later, she allowed him to lead her back to the subway entrance with a promise that she would bring him something more for Christmas.

The following Monday she went to a lawyer in New Rochelle, paid him two hundred dollars, and received some forms for Thomas to sign. She took them to Brooklyn.

Thomas lived in a rundown welfare hotel. Loris felt saliva gathering in her mouth and she wanted desperately to spit as she waited in the urine-soaked hallway for Thomas to come to the door. When he finally did, she told him she couldn't stay long. She had to fend off his advances, but finally she managed to get him to sign the forms for a hundred dollars and her promise that she would come back to see him. Then Loris, her heart beating lighter, smiled practically all the way back to New Rochelle. She took the forms straight to the lawyer's office and he promised to file them the next day.

"You'll get your green card," he promised. And Loris believed him. He had told her about a number of West Indians whom he had helped. He had shown her their letters of thanks, and she was impressed.

"Anyway," she told Selena, "you have to trust somebody sometime. I can't believe God will make me go through this misery again."

The day before Christmas Eve, feeling happy and free for the first time in years, Loris wanted to do something nice, something to say thank you, Jesus. She packed a paper bag of food and took it to Brooklyn for Thomas. She had to knock persistently before a woman in a dirty housecoat and pink curlers answered the door and demanded to know who she was and what she wanted.

Loris told her she was an old friend of Thomas's.

"He ain't here," the woman snapped. "And you can't be that old a friend 'cause I ain't never seen you before."

"I've known him since 1968." Loris, regretting her impulse to come, felt foolish.

"And I've known him since 1958. We been married that long."

"Married? You say you're married to Thomas?"

100

"You heard me," the woman said. "Thomas is mah husband. I just come up from Alabama to spend Christmas with him. Don't you come here…"

Loris dropped the bag of groceries and fled.

She didn't remember much about Christmas that year. The holidays passed in a grey blur. She did her work mechanically, her mind on little else but the possibility that the immigration people would find out that Thomas had been married before and would charge him with bigamy. She would be sent back home for sure. What would she tell her mother? How could she ever hold her head up in the road again?

Right after the New Year opened, she went to see the lawyer.

"Don't worry," he told her. "The immigration service is not that thorough."

But Loris was frightened. She had decided to leave the area. Could she get her two hundred back? Sorry, the lawyer told her. The papers had been filed. She'd just have to wait and see.

Loris went a little crazy after that. She figured the immigration would catch her sooner or later so she might as well have a happy time in America. She started going to West Indian parties in the Bronx with Selena, and that's how she'd met Carl.

Carl. She wished she had never danced with him, never listened to him whisper in her ear that he wanted to roll naked on the beach in Manzanilla with her, never promised to go home for Carnival with him. He called her all the time, pressing her to make her reservation for the trip. He had never asked her if she had her green card; he obviously thought she had it. How could she be in this country so long and not have one? How could she have gone home on holiday two years before (as she had told him), if she didn't have it?

Finally, to stop him pestering her, she told him she had made a booking on Eastern to fly out on Carnival Saturday.

Carl was ecstatic. "We breaking down Port-of-Spain, girl," he laughed. "We dancing all night! And on Carnival Sunday, before Panorama, we going down by the sea."

But at night, as Carnival time got close, Loris, lying in bed, was worried. What would she tell him when he came back? He would demand to know why she hadn't met him at home. What lie could she make up? She had to concoct a convincing story. Finally, she got one. She would tell him that when she went to the airport, Eastern told her the plane was full. They had overbooked. She was mad. She had her ticket. She had demanded a seat. They told her they would put her on the next available flight. She had waited in the cold-arse airport all night. Sunday passed and the airline gave her a chit for dinner at the hotel but still couldn't put her on a flight. Monday morning came.

Carnival Monday. She'd thought about him jumping up in steelbands all over town while she was sitting in Kennedy airport with a ticket in her hand. She could hardly stand it. When five o'clock came and she still couldn't get on a flight, she cussed out the ticket agents and went back to New Rochelle. How could Carl doubt her story?

On the Friday he was to leave, he called from the airport to say that he would meet her the following night in a fête at Sparrow's Hide-Away in Petit Valley. She promised to be there.

On Saturday morning, Loris, feeling more depressed than she had ever felt, called Selena and asked her to go with her to Kovets in the White Plains mall. Selena agreed to come by about one and Loris busied herself cleaning the madam's house.

Just before twelve the doorbell rang. She switched off the vacuum cleaner, wondering how Selena had managed to come so early. The bell rang again before she could reach the door, and she shouted, "You think we have a butler here or what?"

She pulled the door open but it wasn't Selena. The postman stood before her, holding a registered letter.

"Sorry," he smiled. "Want to get finished before the snow comes. You Miss Loris Henry?"

Loris nodded her head reluctantly. Only bad news ever came in a registered envelope. The immigration!

"Sign here," the postman told her. She took his pen and scribbled her name, her hand trembling. He ripped off the return receipt, pushed the letter and the rest of the mail into her hand, and was gone.

Slowly, Loris closed the door and made her way back to the kitchen. She placed the Ames's mail in a basket and put her registered letter on the table. She sat staring at the white legal-looking envelope before her, too frightened to open it, her mind conjuring up the terrible spectre of deportation. She didn't hear Mrs. Ames come into the room until the madam had called her name twice.

"Was that the mailman, Loris?" Mrs. Ames was saying. "Did he bring a box?"

Loris came out of her stupor. "No. I mean yes, Madam. Was the postman. But he didn't have a box. He had this registered letter for me."

"Well, aren't you going to open it?" Mrs. Ames was flipping through her own mail. "Might be important."

Yes, Loris thought. It's important. Immigration and Naturalization Service was stamped clearly on the white envelope.

Mrs. Ames, sensing that something was wrong, took up the letter. "I can open it for you if you'd like, Loris," she said gently. "Whatever the news, you'll have to know sometime." She slit open the envelope with the scissors she carried in her gardening apron. Loris could not watch as Mrs. Ames withdrew the letter and began to read silently.

"But this is excellent news, Loris!" Mrs. Ames said. "The immigration service has written to tell you that your application for a permanent visa has been approved and you are to go to Montreal on March third for an appointment with the American Consul. Look. It says here you're to bring some documents..."

"What document?" Loris cried. "I don't have any..."

"Oh, nothing much. They want to see your passport, of course, but if you don't have that, your birth certificate will do. And they want you to show evidence that you are gainfully employed and that you've been paying taxes."

"But I..." Loris stammered.

"Mister Ames and I would gladly give you a letter confirming your employment," Mrs. Ames was saying. "Hum... mm. Says here such a letter has to be notarized. Well, no problem. We'll get that done." She handed the letter to Loris.

"Now put this away carefully. You must take it with you to the Consulate. There's a number on it. Your number." She picked up her scissors and went back to the sunroom to her plants, leaving Loris lost in wonder.

They had approved her application! The lawyer was right. She would get her green card. Oh God! She would get her green card! Next year she would be able to go home for Carnival. She and Carl...

And slowly, as the meaning of the letter registered on her consciousness, a smile spread across Loris' face, a radiant smile, filling up her eyes, bursting through her cheeks, and she felt like singing a calypso.

HABANA LIBRE

It is Friday. Through narrow back streets washed by an early morning sun, past skyscrapers draped with green fishnets to catch peeling Italian tiles, Marilita Mendoza makes her way towards a factory in the cul-de-sac two blocks down from the back door of the *Habana Libre*. At the hotel's open kitchen door she stops to peer into its dimly lit interior. A warm blast of diesel and cabbage fumes hits her. She exhales in disgust. It is always the same, she thinks, cabbage, diesel, a sameness regardless of what is bubbling on the stove. Marilita turns her head to catch a clear breath before her lips form the whistle that will summon Rico. When he does not answer the signal, she calls softly, urgently, Rico? Rico?

No one answers.

She leans against the dry-rotted doorpost to slip off her right shoe. With it she knocks on the door twice, then once, then once again. A thin man appears. Marilita recognizes the cook in his baggy black pants and bloodstained apron. She bends her head and pretends to be fixing her shoe heel. The cook demands to know what she wants. Pointing to a slightly protruding nail in the heel, she asks him to lend her a hammer. He flaps his dingy towel as he would swat a mosquito, and orders her away. She slips on her shoe. She straightens up slowly. Then she tosses her head back and moves down the alley straight and tall as if she is carrying a full bucket of water on her head. When she can no longer feel the cook's eyes on her, she turns and spits a curse at him and all his foul descendants, but he is no longer in the doorway.

Marilita is worried. Where is Rico? What's happened to him? Why is he not in the kitchen washing dishes, sweeping the floor, peeling potatoes? Every week, day-in day-out for the six months she has known him, he's been there. He must be sick. But he was well yesterday. He'd come to the door. He'd told her they were in luck. Mañana, he had said, mañana he would have good news. He had made a contact. He would know more that night. He would tell her on Friday. "Be ready," he had said. "Any time soon." Something bad must have happened to him. And that damn cook. Ai! He would never answer her questions. Perhaps Rico had missed his bus. Perhaps the bus broke down. She should have known something would go wrong. Hadn't she stubbed the big toe of her right foot on that pile of stones as she came out her front door this morning? Ai… ai… yi! And her right eye has been jumping since last night.

She's at the door of the factory whispering "Hail Marys" while comrades wish her good morning. Her lips smile in response, but her heart is heavy with worry. What good is a morning when your life is in the palms of a missing man's hands? She reaches her work station. As bad luck would have it, Carmen, who shares her table, is already on her stool fidgeting with a knot in the blue scarf she ties around her head each morning.

"Ummmhummm," Carmen smiles wickedly. "You're praying again, amiga. I see it in your face. Not to worry. I will say nothing! But you must promise to send me a scarf of orange and green. Not blue. I hate blue."

Marilita squeezes Carmen's knee. Then, as Señora Urqualo, the Directora, enters the factory's mail room from her side office, Marilita and Carmen each lift a wire basket to the top of the table and begin to work. Senor Urqualo approaches their table and Marilita's heart skips two beats.

How could she know? Carmen! Carmen has told her! Trust no one, her father had warned her. No. Carmen would not do that. Carmen knows how she feels. Rico. Something has happened. Oh Madre de Dios! Madre de Dios!

"It is your turn to post the *Granma*," Señora Urqualo is saying. "You continue to neglect your duties."

Marilita begs her pardon, slips off her stool, and takes the newspaper from the Directora's outstretched hand. As quickly as she can, she pins its pages on the bulletin board across from the work tables.

"Bueno," Senora Urqualo tells her. "You will do it again next

Friday. Try not to let your mind wander so much, Marilita. It is not a good thing. You make your father very unhappy."

And what of my happiness? Marilita screams inside as she smiles an apology. Rico is gone! I should care about my father? He has his happiness.

"You may return to your table. And make no more mistakes today."

Make no mistakes? What is there to know any more about twisting wire around wire. She had asked this of her father when he had proudly announced that he had secured this position for her. His long arms had swept the air in a proud embrace as he told her of the benefits of steady employment in a position protected by the Party. You must join, he had insisted. Life will be good for you. We Party members. It is we who live the glory of the revolution. It is through our will, our example, that oppressed people all over the world may know how to live free. But she had begun to block his words with images of her mother swimming the water off the Malécon with a fish in her teeth. Her mother. So brave. So daring! What courage she must have had to leave her child, her husband… Her father, seeing the glaze in her eyes, had drawn her close to him to him to whisper prayers to Erzulie to whom he had been praying for eighteen years for help with his marooned child.

Marilita is holding a doll, a ballerina, in her left hand. She selects a pink strip of wire from a section of the basket in front of her, and begins to wind it around the wire legs of the ballerina. Pink tights for a white ballerina – she has memorized her instructions. On Friday we make dancers. Folk dancers with black faces get black tights. Ballet dancers with white faces get pink tights, and white tutus. When you are finished with the tights, pass the doll to Carmen. She will slip on the tutu. She will bend the wire arms in a graceful posture. She will tip the feet and bend one knee. And Lolla, at the next table, will paint red lips and rouge its cheek, and place a crown on its head. I will then place it on its stand: "The New Cuban Woman". On Thursday we make the New Cuban Man. Dark-skinned schoolboys. Every Cuban a literate person! You, Marilita, will put on his hat with its little beak like a hummingbird's, and you will sling his cardboard bookbag across his shoulder, just so, and then you will pass him to Carmen, and she will glue him to his pedestal before she polishes him and places him in his box marked for the tourist shop at the *Habana Libre*.

One Monday, a long half year ago, she had followed Señora Urqualo's orders to take a filled box of dolls to the hotel. As instructed, she had passed through the back door, through the kitchen, and Rico had raised his head from his potato peeling to wink at her. Ai, yi, ah yi! You will know when it happens, her father had told her. You will hear music no one else hears. And so she had waited for him, knowing he would come to the bus stop to see her even though not a word passed between them as she had gone in and out of the *Habana Libre* that day. And where was he now? What has happened to cause him to miss work? Was his sister sick? He has never taken her to his sister's house, but he has told her all about Juanita and her five children, whose father has run off to Miami. She is all the family he has left. He takes care of her and the children. Their apartment is small. One bedroom for so many people. He sleeps on the floor of the front room. It is no place to take a girlfriend. So for months they walk along the Malécon, pressing their needs together against the sea wall, sucking each other's tongues, hungry for each other's bodies, but she had said no, not so. They must wait. And she had known, absolutely, that he was the one because, unlike those others, he had said Sí, Sí. We will wait.

Carmen's laughter had rung loudly across the park when Marilita had told her how she and Rico spent their time together. "You spend your aching hours eating ice cream and nibbling each other's ears? What is the point of waiting? When will you qualify for an apartment? There are hundreds ahead of you. You have joined the Party, but so have they. I know a place, Marilita. I will show you. Live now. Take your fun this moment. It is as private as you can get in Habana. It's in a cove. Wednesday night is best. Only a few couples go there then, and they will not trouble you. Take a blanket." And Carmen had dragged her off one evening to the place, and she had told Rico about it but they had never used it until last Wednesday night. Rico's birthday. Twenty-two. And what could she give him that was precious?

108

Her father had said he had spoken to the district chairman who had made another notation against her and Rico's names. As soon as even a room became available, they would be in line for it. Party members are always first, her father had assured her. How many thousands had been so assured, Marilita had asked. Her father had begged her to have patience. All Cubans must have patience. It is the essence of patriotism.

The world is spinning slowly and Marilita times its movement with the shifting of the sun's rays through the jalousies on the east side of the factory. She tries hard to push against it but the heaviness in her mind descends to the fringes of her heart as her fingers keep a steady rendezvous with the familiar rhythm: wrap wrap wrap wrap wrap wrap wrap wrap bend... take another pink strip, wrap wrap wrap wrap wrap wrap wrap wrap bend... take another... pink... He had held her so tightly as they had walked back to her bus stop from the cove. "I will never love another woman in my life," he had promised, and with his kisses on her lips, on her neck and throat punctuating each word, "I promise you, Marilita, wherever I am, you will be too... Madre de Dios. He could *not* have been lying. She would have known. A woman knows these things.

She must find him. She will search the whole of Habana until she finds his sister's place. His sister. Was that a lie? He had shown her no photo of this sister nor of her children. She will make a novena on his head. She will place the blessed stones on her windowsill as soon as she reaches home, and she will pray his name to all the orishas, to all the saints... wrap wrap wrap wrap wrap wrap wrap wrap bend... take another pink...

Midmorning air hangs heavy in the factory, and once, when she grumbles a complaint to Carmen about the only fan being near the Directora's desk, Carmen suggests that she should be thankful that she was not recruited to cut the canes this season for "That is hot, amiga!"

A little later, Marilita asks the Directora's permission to use the toilet. Pressure has a vice-grip on her insides and it is with tremendous relief that she opens the door. She latches it, sinks with relief onto the seat, and wishes she could stay in long enough to relieve herself of all her fears, but Señora Urqualo keeps a strict watch. There is no toilet paper so Marilita tears a piece of last week's *Granma*, dampens it from the bottle of water in the corner – for the faucet is broken – and wipes herself. She flushes, but the newspaper floats to the top, and here again is evidence of her bad luck. Who will Señora Urqualo blame for clogging the toilet? Ai!

Near noon, the sun no longer comes into the factory, for there are no openings to the west. Marilita summons good thoughts of Rico to replace the despair. Sí. He will be there. In the kitchen. When she checks at noon. Enough! Attend to the work. She focuses, then, on the slow, steady rhythm of her comrades' hands as they wrap and bend and form the kaleidoscope of new Cuban images. She reads stories in the women's hands. Blight. Blight is sucking their bodies of all possibilities. They are the living dead. Look at table two… Consuelo, Tita… their bodies bent over. What do they have to think about? Do they have a Rico to whom they have entrusted the living part of their souls so they can be shells in this factory? Patience. Her father had advised her. You could learn from these women, Marilita. They know what it means to be part of the struggle against the greatest power in the world, and to survive! To refuse to be crushed! These women have a hard life, Marilita, but who has caused this hardship, eh? Have patience.

"Ding!" Señora Urqualo has pressed the table bell which she, as a district captain, had confiscated from the front desk of the *Hilton Hotel* during the revolution. Marilita and Carmen and their comrades bed the figures and the wires and the beads in their separate boxes, each trying not to appear too eager to abandon her post.

Once outside the factory, and away from the Directora's watchful eyes, Marilita slips away from Carmen and the others. She hurries up the alley toward the *Habana Libre*. She has fifteen minutes for lunch. Fifteen minutes to check on Rico at work, and if he is still not there, she must race down by the sea wall. Her steps are fast and hard and the nail in her shoe presses against her sole so she takes off both shoes and carries them under her arm. What does she care? Everybody in Habana knows that shoes are often too tight or too loose a fit.

On a sudden impulse, she decides to go around to the front of the hotel to inquire about Rico. Quickly, she washes her feet under a standpipe in the alley, dons her shoes, and bemoans the white threads that show in the front and side seams of her too tight brown bell-bottoms. She knows she will fool no one. She is not a turista, and her entry would be certain to attract attention. So? What does she have to lose? She who has lost all already. She will dare to enter the hotel from the front!

The eyes of the two taxi drivers lingering in front of the dry fountain turn, simultaneously, to stare as Marilita Mendoza, her neck stretched defiantly, shoulders back, chest thrust forward, goosesteps into the lobby of the *Habana Libre*, and up to its reception desk. Oi! Diesel! Cabbage! Even in the front! Dizziness sweeps up in her as the whole of Habana explodes in her stomach. She steadies herself at the counter.

"No," the white-haired clerk is firm. He cannot allow her to go through to the kitchen to check on Rico.

"Señor..." Marilita begins, and slumps to the floor. The doorman and the bellhop rush to lift her bony frame to the side chair, out of sight of the Canadians registering. The clerk's quarrelsome voice diagnoses her as a starving *angustia* who must be seeking food from Rico. He instructs the bellhop to fan her with a folded *Granma*, and sends the doorman to the back in search of Rico. Marilita allows her eyelids to flicker momentarily when the doorman returns to announce that Rico is not at his post. A cup of water is forced to Marilita's lips, and a taxi driver summoned to take her to hospital.

Marilita allows herself to be placed in the back seat of the taxi. She remains still until she knows they are well away from the hotel. Then she rises and taps the driver on his shoulder. "The Malécon, Señor?" she says weakly. "Some sea air will do me better than a long wait in the hospital."

The driver shrugs his shoulders. What does he care about this crazy woman who must surely be from the interior? Who else but a country fool would not know the rules? Glad to be rid of her, he returns to the hotel to await a real passenger.

Marilita waits until the taxi is out of sight before she walks along the sea wall hoping to see one of Rico's friends fishing. The rough waves splash high against slippery rocks below the breakway and she chides herself for not remembering that it is not a day for fishing. Ai… ai… yi! Look at the sky! Pink scales in the clouds. Who could catch fish along the Malécon on a day like this? And see the sun. Time has stopped crawling across Habana today. Run. Forget the hunger pains in my belly. Forget the pain in my head. Better run before Señora Urqualo opens her ledger!

After five, on her way home, Marilita pauses by the back door of the *Habana Libre* even though she is convinced Rico will not be there. A woman Marilita recognizes as part of the kitchen help is lingering over the garbage heap, dragging smoke from a cigarette butt. She tells Marilita that Rico will be replaced the next day by the cook's nephew.

"But where has he gone?" Marilita pleads.

The woman shrugs her shoulders.

"Señora, please," Marilita touches the woman's arm. "Por favor. Was he sent to cut the canes? You must tell me! Por favor, por favor."

The woman flicks the last of her cigarette's ash into the garbage, and goes into the kitchen.

"Bitch!" Marilita screams. "Crabs will eat your husband's balls!" She makes a furious sign of the cross with her right hand to ward off the woman's evil aura as she hurries up the alley.

A sliver of hope lingers to torment her. On the crowded bus she sees the back of Rico's head far at the rear but when he turns, the face is a stranger's. And another, wearing Rico's mauve striped shirt with his hairy arms clinging to the worn bus-strap, has a tattooed scorpion on his wrist to distinguish him from Rico. Heaviness closes about her heart. Bile crawls up from her navel to her throat. She wants to spit at these two men.

Home, in the small third-floor apartment, she fries two eggs and a plantain, dips out a little for herself, but leaves most of it covered with an aluminium pan on the table for her father. She forces herself to eat her small portion, but food will not satisfy her emptiness. She scrapes her plate over the dustbin, rinses it and her fork, and places them to drain on the counter. Then she turns up the faucet, leans over the kitchen sink and squishes water between the cracks in her teeth to find and dislodge any specks of egg. She hates eggs. She eats them because eggs are the only source of protein available in the stores these days, and her father insists that her bones will decay without some nourishment. She washes her face, dries it with the palms of her hands, before she goes back to the streets to search for Rico.

Friday night. Habana is hopping. Young men and young women cling to each other as they move as one from ice cream stands to movie houses or to the Malécon in search of a private spot. Marilita watches them. She walks and she stares and she speaks with her eyes to the girls: Don't listen to his lies. He will bite the softness in your ear and he will whisper that he will never leave you. He will spoon vanilla ice cream between your lips and you will suck his tongue and his hands will trace his need across your nipples and he will swear that he will find a way for you to be together for good. Like you, he is tired of being patient. You want to leave. Sí. He wants to leave too. And he will tell you that you will go together. He has good news. A Canadian *turista* at the *Habana Libre* has taken a message he will send to your mother in Miami. His fingers will rake the curls around your *michita* and he will murmur that arrangements are being made for both of you, for how can he ever separate himself from your ecstasy? He will take your savings to pay the fisherman who will arrange for both of you to get to Miami, and you will believe him and you will tell your mother when you get to Miami that you knew he was the one when he first winked at you, and because never before had you tasted such sweetness as when he entered you, and you knew it was the same for him last Wednesday.

The last bus from the city to Marilita's district leaves at ten past midnight and she wearily but reluctantly boards it. The driver is the same one she had smiled at last Wednesday after Rico had kissed her at the bus stop. Marilita avoids his eyes. She wants to sit far away from him but three couples sit at the rear waiting, Marilita knows, for the folding doors to close and the lights to dim so they can reach fingers into brassieres and drawers and hide their eagerness with giggles. She sits down behind the driver, grateful for the Plexiglas partitioning them, but she knows what he is thinking. She knows he is smiling. He has seen her face, her downcast eyes. He can tell. He will go home to his wife and tell

113

her about the girl who last Wednesday had been so happy. *La vida loca!* Then he will laugh. But what does he know of hope? The sameness of his life has robbed him of the pleasure and pain of being alive. He is like the women in the factory, zombies, all of them. So, Rico has gone. Maybe he's been sent to cut canes, maybe he has slipped away to Miami. But wherever he is, he *cannot* forget her. On this, she decides, she will rebuild her faith. She looks out of the window at the new moon. The woman on her broomstick is dancing round and round her dog. It is always like this, she knows, when good luck is on its way.

PELAU

First you have to decide if you making chicken or beef pelau. Either way, you have to cut up the meat and wash it good with limes or lemons or grapefruits – if that is all you have – before you season it down good with thyme, tomatoes, onions, chives – a fresh bunch of bouquet garni will work good – and salt and pepper. You have to do this overnight for the seasoning to set into the meat. I like to do mine two days in advance and store it in a bowl in the fridge.

Next day, put a big pot – iron pot if you have one – with some oil in it, on the fire to heat up. Throw in a handful of white sugar; low down the fire, and let the sugar burn brown. You have to watch the sugar burning to keep it from smoking up the house.

After the sugar turn a dark brown – don't let it burn hard – add the meat slow slow, turning it every once in a while to get all the pieces nice and dark. Throw in all the seasoning and whatever water is in the bowl. Cover the pot. Let that cook for about twenty minutes, depending on how much meat is in the pot, until the meat feel tender and nice. You could add a little salt and pepper now, depending on your taste. I like to put in a whole bird pepper but not everybody like their food hot like me.

Depending on how much rice you want to cook, add three to four cups of water. All the water have to evaporate in the rice so you going to have to watch the pot while it cooking.

Is best to put on some calypso music and shuffle your feet while you waiting for the water to boil up.

When you see the water bubbling, throw in the rice. Now some people like to wash their rice beforehand, but I never do that because that is washing half the strength away. I must be doing something right because I'm ninety-four and I ent dead yet. What don't kill will fatten.

Make sure water covering the rice and chicken with about a cup to spare. You need to taste it after stirring to make sure it have enough salt.

Some people like to add pigeon peas, or some cut-up carrots. That's all well and good; just make sure if the peas come from a can, rinse them off before putting them in the pot. Throw away the water they come in in the can. Stir to make sure the rice and meat and everything mix up good, and you have enough water to cook it all down. If you want, you could add a little bit of butter before you cover the pot, and turn the fire down low.

A lot of people's pelau does burn because they don't know this little trick:

Turn the pot cover upside down and put some water in it. If by chance the water in the pot dry down, that little bit in the pot cover will keep the rice from burning, but you need to lift the cover and check how the rice cooking, every ten minutes or so. In about half-hour, the food done. You could serve it right away with a nice piece of zabocca on the side, but pelau does really taste better the day after you cook it.

ON A POINT OF ORDER

In the early afternoon, just when the school children were making their way home, a loudspeaker van swung into the village, and Ramkesoon's voice came crackling over the system: "Come one! Come all! Free film show tonight at your community centre. The Bagatelle Village Council cordially invites you to a free film show brought to you specially from New York."

Ramkesoon threw sweets and bubble gum to the waving school children, then ordered his driver to swing off the dirt road. The driver smiled knowingly. He did not protest even though he knew they would be breaking their boss's specific orders to stay on the Main Road. Just before they had driven out of the yard, the boss had reminded them about the van they had nearly run over a precipice the week before, when, against orders, they had gone down a narrow side road, and then couldn't turn the van around.

"Is only one van I have left," the boss had warned. "All you don't go in de village showing off to dem girls, playing all you is cowboys, and break down my van. Is trouble in all you arse if dat happen, oui!"

But Ramkesoon and the driver *were* cowboys. They were the Lone Ranger and Tonto, the Cisco Kid and Poncho, Roy Rogers and Trigger. They knew every cowboy move – the quick draw, the slit eyes, the smirk. They rode through the village, pretending it was the range, and took chances as they knew all cowboys did in the movies. They were rewarded with shy smiles from the village girls, and welcoming handshakes from the men. Then they swung stylishly out of the village, parked the truck, and went into the rumshop – the watering hole, as Ramkesoon called it – to drink with the fellars until it was time to return the van to the yard, and mosey on over to the community centre for the film show.

117

The film was to be shown after the monthly village council meeting. The villagers gathered early to get good seats, but the meeting began late. About nine-thirty the president entered the community centre and nodded to a few people who acknowledged his arrival with shouts of "Is time you get here, man," and, "Start de meeting, man, Francis. It hot like hell in here." Francis took off his Panama hat, fanned his face with it a few times, then hung it on the nail reserved exclusively for it behind the officers' table. He flopped into his chair between Miss Dorothy, the secretary, and Mr. Henry, the treasurer, glanced at the vacant vice-president's chair, and with some annoyance, asked Miss Dorothy, "You mean to say Barrow late again?"

Miss Dorothy stopped her perusal of the minutes, looked at her watch, and said, "You know, Mr. President, it seem to me that we have a case of de pot calling de kettle black. You is de one who always comin' late, not Barrow. Besides, Barrow's not late. He was here but he had to go up de hill to borrow an extension cord."

"What he need extension cord for?" Francis asked.

"But how you so forgetful, Mister President? I thought I tell you last week dat de people comin' to give a show tonight?" Miss Dorothy was obviously exasperated.

"But why you have to get so huffy and puffy? You mean I can't ask a question?" Francis was indignant. He knew Miss Dorothy resented him as President, a post she had craved. He had won the last election by only three votes and he had heard that she had gone about the village accusing him of cheating. He felt that she took pleasure, at every opportunity, in publicly humiliating him.

He told her haughtily, "You expect me to remember foolishness like film show? Dat's your job!" And before Miss Dorothy could answer he banged his hammer on the table and called out to the packed room, "De meeting will now come to order. Everybody sit down. Who can't sit down, lean against the walls. Come on all you, move away from de door, man. Ramkesoon, Tyrone, you blocking de little bit ah wind from comin through. Move aside, man."

People shuffled about trying to find a convenient spot to lean against. Ramkesoon planted himself in a corner and refused to move for people to get by him. A few boys blocked the two

118

windows in the one-room building, and those who were trying to peer in swore and shouted to the president to make them move.

Francis shouted for order. He nodded to Miss Dorothy to begin.

Miss Dorothy rose, smoothed her blue taffeta skirt, cleared her throat, and in shrill falsetto began to sing the opening song, "Bless This House", a cappella.

Francis sighed. He had tried unsuccessfully for two years to dissuade Miss Dorothy from singing that song. The words, he thought, were most inappropriate.

The very walls Miss Dorothy was earnestly asking the Lord to preserve were crumbling from severe attacks by termites. They were made from wood donated to the village council by the Americans. Barrow, the vice-president, worked at the American base as a bar man, and he had begged the American colonel for the wood for the community centre. The Americans were in the process of building more permanent quarters so they were happy to donate the old wood to the council. That was two years ago. Since then, the one-room centre, covered with rusty galvanized sheets, had taken just about all it could from the rain, wind, insects, and the village children who constantly broke off pieces of the wood to use as cricket bats. The Village Council had sent several letters to the central office in the city requesting money to fix the centre, but even after the Prime Minister had come to inspect the place, their requests were ignored. Francis had a theory about that. He felt that the central office was displeased with the officers and members of the village council because, by begging the Americans for the wood, the council had embarrassed the Prime Minister who had just been demanding the return of the land on which the Americans had built their base.

Miss Dorothy sang, "Bless the people here within, Keep them free from shame and sin." Francis sucked his teeth in disgust. The song was an embarrassment to him personally, and he had asked, no, pleaded with Miss Dorothy to try a different tune, but she ignored him. Miss Dorothy saw herself as a mediator, an intercessor, a woman who took her responsibilities for the community very seriously. She considered it her duty, her calling, to plead the cause of her fellow villagers as often as possible. She used to be

119

able to do it in the Anglican church where, she was convinced, the Lord was more inclined to listen, but she had been relieved of her position as soloist for the choir when a new priest took over. Miss Dorothy had not taken her dismissal with Christian humility. She had written to the bishop about it. He had not replied. But then the priest's young wife, a woman who, much to the dismay of the parishioners, favoured low-cut, sleeveless dresses, left him to return to England. The official story was that she could not stand the climate, but Miss Dorothy knew better. There had been an anonymous letter to the bishop, revealing certain amorous adventures the lady had had with a young man in the village. Miss Dorothy was sure that it was only a matter of time before her husband would follow her. Until then, however, she had to content herself with the twice-monthly rendition of "Bless This House" in the community centre. She had selected the song carefully. She felt that it set the right mood for the meeting. As always, she held the final note as long as she could and then sat down.

The audience, accustomed as it was to the performance, did not applaud. Barrow arrived as Miss Dorothy finished and, walking down the aisle to the officers' table with an extension cord in his hand, thought it fitting to proclaim, "Amen!" Ramkesoon stamped loudly. His legs were getting heavy with cramp, and he wished fervently for the meeting to end. As he had told his friend earlier, "I only going for de film show, oui. I not in all dat village council bacchanal."

Francis mopped his forehead with a dingy handkerchief, checked the handwritten agenda, and announced, "De secretary will now read de minutes."

Miss Dorothy reached for the pages she had placed on the table when she had risen to sing. They were not there. "Where de minutes gone?" she asked.

"Dey right here." The treasurer handed the pages to her.

Miss Dorothy snatched them from him and rose.

"Mister President, officers and members of de village council, distinguished guests, ladies and gentlemen. Dese are de minutes of de last meetin of the Bagatelle Village Council held on de thirtyut' day of June, 1969, at de community centre, Diego Martin, Trinidad, West Indies." She paused to slap a brave mosquito that had landed on the page, and in that pause a voice cried out from the audience: "Mister President, on ah point of order, please."

Francis failed to respond. He was, in fact, asleep. Barrow hit Francis' knee under the table and Francis came awake with a start. The voice rang out again.

"Mister President, like you ain't hear me or what? I say on ah point of order, please."

Francis blinked, peered out at the man standing with his hand raised, and said, "Make your point, Superville."

"But Mister President," Miss Dorothy protested, "I have de floor."

"Sit down, Dorothy," Francis said. "I giving Superville de floor."

Miss Dorothy huffed but she sat.

Superville said, "Mister President, I want to make ah motion."

"Well, make de motion, man," Francis said. "You waitin' till cock get teeth?"

"De motion I want to make, Mister President, officers and members, is dat we don't bother with de reading of de minutes tonight. De meeting start so late already, I feel that we should put off reading de minutes till next time. It getting real late and we want to see de show."

Several voices in the audience murmured agreement. The president looked at the vice-president. The vice-president shrugged his shoulders. The president looked across at Miss Dorothy. Miss Dorothy turned to gaze deliberately at a framed picture of Queen Elizabeth on the wall.

Henry, the treasurer, asked, "Superville, you mean you want us to have two sets of minutes to listen to next meeting?" It was obvious from Henry's tone that the mere thought was enough to make him sick. He was, after all, a man of figures, not words.

"Not really," said Superville.

"Well, what you mean, den?"

"Well, what I mean is, I been really thinking bout dis whole minutes thing for ah long time now."

The president rapped his hammer on the table. He said, "Superville, if you have something to say, say it. We don't have all night here."

A fellow at the back of the room shouted, "Yes, man, hurry up and make your point. Mosquitoes killing me here!"

Superville rushed on. "Mister President, I just think we does waste too much time reading minutes. I was saying so to some of de other members de other day and we come up with de idea that maybe we shouldn't have reading of de minutes any more. We all know what happen already. Why we have to hear it again? And if somebody miss ah meeting, all he have to do is ask somebody who was dere."

"De man have ah point!" Ramkesoon shouted.

The president banged his hammer on the table. "Too much people talking one time. Superville, what is your motion again?"

Superville said, "I make de motion dat we don't read minutes at de meetin any more."

"Dat don't sound like de same motion you make before, Superville," Henry said.

"I second dat!" a voice from the window shouted.

"What you seconding, de motion or de statement?" the president asked the voice, and muttered, "Fool."

"Is me," the voice identified itself. "Is me, Glendora, Mister Charlie's daughter. I second de motion. We don't need no stale news."

"Okay," Francis said. "We have a motion on de floor, placed by Superville, seconded by Glendora, dat we shouldn't read de minutes at village council meetings. Anybody have anything to say to dat? Superville, you could sit down now."

A hand was raised from the second row.

"De chair recognizes Lionel Bartholomew. Bart, what you want?" Francis said.

Lionel Bartholomew stood on his toes. He was a small man who never appeared in public without a white shirt, a suit, and a tie. He had come to the village ten years before with three broken-down typewriters and a small brown grip packed with papers. He told everyone he had been to England to study Pitman's shorthand and typing. He rented two rooms from Miss Dorothy, lived in one, and set up Bartholomew's Commercial School in the other. Since he had only three typewriters, none of which worked, he had few students. But over the years he had managed to make enough to pay his rent, and pay Miss Dorothy to wash and iron his white shirts by giving private lessons in English language and literature (he pronounced it litterrahture) to children.

"I rise, Mister President," Bartholomew said in his most precise accent, "on a point of order." He spoke, he had often told the villagers, only the Queen's English.

Miss Dorothy scribbled quickly in her notebook, Henry stared at his figures, and the president pulled out his handkerchief to swat a mosquito. They all knew no good would come by trying to hurry Bartholomew. He always took his time.

"I wish," Bartholomew continued, "to speak to the motion recently placed on the floor." Here he paused, reached for a small black book that he always brought to the meetings, and flipped the pages. When he had found the page he wanted, he once more addressed the president.

"Mister President, I have here in my possession a copy of Roberts' Rules of Order, published by the order of Her Majesty, in London, England." Bartholomew rocked back on his heels, straightened his tie, and tipped forward again.

"This book, Mister President, contains the precise rules and procedures we are to follow. This is parliamentary procedure." He held the book high. "These rules were set in the Mother Country and commissioned by Her Majesty herself. Under the section entitled 'Minutes" it says, and I quote, 'the minutes are read at the opening of each day's meeting, and, after correction, should be approved,' end of quote, page 249. Now I ask you, Mister President, how can we possibly agree to discontinue the reading of the minutes? That would be like slapping the Queen in her face. I simply cannot allow it."

Miss Dorothy rubbed her lower lip and smiled. She decided she would have to put a little more starch in Bart's shirts.

Francis looked at his watch. It said five minutes before ten. He looked at Bartholomew. He said, "Bart, when was de last time a mosquito bite you on your neck?"

"I do not see what mosquitoes have to do with this, Mister President," Bartholomew said.

The president lashed out at another mosquito that had burst

into song as it danced about his head. "Well, I tell you something, Bart," he said. "Dey have ah hell of ah lot to do with it. You see, de longer we stay here, de more mosquito bites we all going to get. And I don't know 'bout you, but I have enough razor bumps on my face and neck. I don't need no mosquito bumps. So what I going to do is ask you to sit down and call for ah vote on de motion. All in favour of no meetings I mean, no minutes reading at de meeting, say aye."

A chorus of "ayes" went up. Bartholomew shouted, "I object, Mister President, I object and I rise on a point of order!"

Francis banged his hammer twice on the table. "Sit down, Bart. We trying to take a vote here. All not in favour of de motion say no."

Bartholomew and Miss Dorothy shouted in unison, "No!"

"The ayes have it,'" Francis shouted. "Make ah note of dat, Madam Secretary. Now, de next item on de agenda is de showing of de film."

Bartholomew was still standing, loudly protesting the vote. The president told him, "Bart, if you don't take your seat I'm going to have to fine you ah dollar for disrupting de meeting. Now sit your tail down!"

Bartholomew plunked his hat on his head and stalked out of the centre.

"As I was saying," Francis said, "de next item on de agenda is a showing of de film entitled 'De Good, de Bad, and de Ugly" starring the famous… ah… who it starring again?" He turned to Miss Dorothy, but she had turned her back on him.

Ramkesoon shouted "Clint Eastwood!" And Barrow said, "Well, yes, Mr. Clint Eastwood. Dis film coming to you from de United States Information Service. Barrow, you have de extension cord? Okay, everybody, settle down. Somebody douse de lights dere. Everybody keep quiet."

Ramkesoon smiled and settled back against the wall to enjoy the film show.

A YELLOW ROSE IN TEXAS

On the Sunday after they got paid, right after Mrs. Charles, dressed-up in her best flowered hat, chiffon dress, and Guyana gold slave-bands adorning her wrist, had departed for church, Velma and Diane carefully removed the cream crocheted table cloth from the mahogany dining table. Standing at opposite ends, they folded the table cloth between them so it wouldn't crease, and hung it over the back of a side chair before sitting down with pens and paper, to write letters to their families back home.

The writing wasn't easy. After the first truths, new ones had to be invented. Velma and Diane had no trouble with the address, the date, the salutation and comma after it, but then came the body. That was the difficult part. They would rest their pens down on the table and gaze into space, hoping for the right words to appear in front of them, having exhausted their supply of adjectives with which to describe New York.

Caught up in the excitement of newness just after she arrived, Velma had not been able to understand why the houses – or Brownstones as people on St. John's Place in Brooklyn called them – *didn't even have enough space to plant one row of beans between them. With a tiny backyard no bigger than a twenty-cent stamp, no wonder the children played in the streets morning, noon and night – and it was a wonder that they didn't get knocked down. And the cars? Lord Ma! So many cars you would think everybody in New York must own at least two, but that's not true. A lot of them don't even own one. Don't tell Miss Ann this, you know how she likes to boast about her family in America, but her sister, Marie, where I'm staying in Brooklyn, can't even afford a car. And if you see how they're living! The apartment has two bedrooms and it's nine of them staying in it.*

West Indians are living one on top of each other in this place. But Marie says they are saving to buy a house in Queens, a nicer part of New York.

The wonder of ready-made clothes and shoes to match, every colour dress you could ever dream of wearing, had held Diane's interest for weeks. But even more amazing than the variety was the fact that she could buy a dress, wear it, find fault with it, return it to the store, and still get her money back! Only in America! Then there was the food.

To Velma, the food tasted bad, too bad. *No seasoning at all. I went to buy chicken in the supermarket – they have giant supermarkets here, like HI-LO, only bigger – and when I got home with this dead chicken wrapped up in plastic? No blood! "Where the blood gone?" I asked. Somewhere in America they're growing chickens without blood. I've never seen anything like that. I couldn't eat it. I had to throw it in the garbage. Most days, I have to close my eyes to eat this food over here.*

Tell Clive that the trucks are really big. You have to wait ten minutes to cross the road when one's passing. And the trains go down under the ground.

Fascinated by the styles American girls wore, Diane adored the minute details of their revealing skirts and huge Afros. *They say Black people shouldn't press their hair anymore. Black is beautiful, so all the girls are wearing their hair like Africans.*

Having suffered heat waves and burns on their foreheads, ear lobes, and necks, from hot combs, every Saturday back home, both girls contemplated changing to Afros but neither would admit that to the folks back home. After all, they knew when people in Trinidad said, "Your hair is your beauty" they meant long straight strands, not nappy curls. They laughed together as they imagined the palpitations they would cause in their mothers if they sent down pictures of themselves in Afros.

So they wrote about sidewalk stalls, with laden trays of apples and grapes, fruits that were available in Trinidad only at Christmas time. Never had they seen so many different types and sizes of apples. Even green ones. The bountifulness of it all had sent their pens scribbling across the pages in superlatives.

One Sunday in late October, they took up their pens to write. Diane opened with:

Ma, this month I have to buy a coat because it's getting really cold. I'm sending you a hundred dollars in this letter but I'll send more at the end of the month. How's Shawn doing? He's getting tall? He's learning his lessons? I don't want no duncyhead child, so make him do his schoolwork. You could have Maxwell take a picture of Shawn for me please? Tell Shawn I will call Boxing Day. Go over by Miss Andrews about ten o'clock and wait for me to ring. And check how much it costs to put in a phone, Ma, then write and tell me. I don't like Miss Andrews hearing all my business. Don't worry about me, okay? Everything's fine.

Velma, glancing over, read the last line: "Everything's fine." She pushed her own pen and paper away and took up Diane's letter. "Why we lie to them so much, Dee?" she asked. "Why you think we never tell them how much hell we catching up here?"

Diane shrugged her shoulders. "What good that will do?"

"So you think we doing them some good by not telling them the whole story?"

"I'm not lying," Diane tried to take back her letter, "You see me lying?"

"Okay, so you tell Tante Lill that you have to buy a coat, but you didn't say one word about how you cry when you have to go out in the cold. How your fingers turn blue when you're waiting for the bus."

"And telling Ma that will make it better? Girl, give me meh letter, eh. I have work to do."

When Velma refused to hand over the letter, Diane pointed to her belly, "Why you don't write that? You tell them, nuh, if that makes you happy?" And she grabbed Velma's letter. "You talking about me telling lies? Look what you write. All this stupidness about leaves turning colour. I don't see one word here about your condition. You want to tell the truth? Why you don't write about how Nina Simone fired you?" Diane sucked her teeth. "Don't get me mad this Sunday morning, Velma."

Velma had risen to look out the window into Mrs. Charles's dying garden. "You know full well I can't tell Ma 'bout my condition. And you better keep your promise, Dee. Don't say

127

anything to Tantie Lill either. I don't want them worrying about me."

"But you expect me to tell them thing so they could worry 'bout me? What sense that make?"

"Okay, so some things we shouldn't tell them, but what about how people treat us? I mean, why we never tell them how people on the bus don't give us a smile, not a good morning. They just stare at us as if we come from Mars. And we never tell them how blasted hard we have to work for a little bit of money in this country. Why we making them believe we have life easy up here?"

"Because," Diane shrugged her shoulders, "America is a like a dream. And for them, the dream is what is true. It was that way for us too."

"But it's not right, Dee," Velma said angrily. "We know that the America they're dreaming so hard about is not the real one."

"So you're saying you're sorry you come, right? You wish you could go Trinidad this minute, right?"

"No," Velma shook her head. "I'm not saying that. I have to keep going no matter, but I wonder if I would have come at all if I had known how this place is."

"You think you shoulda listen to Uncle Bob? He never had anything good to say about the States."

"Daddy was always so negative," Velma said, "that I couldn't tell what was true. Besides, Ma said New York was different, and Daddy had only been to Florida."

"Well?' Diane said, "I'm willing to bet that even if somebody HAD told us how ugly this place could be, we would have wanted to see for ourselves. Besides which, we just got here. I've been here what, six months? When we were in Trinidad, we thought New York was America, remember?"

"And Florida," Velma added with a laugh. "New York and Florida made up America."

"Well," Diane went on, "we come to find out there are places called Iowa and Montana and don't forget the Dakotas. I'd love to go there one day. The Dakotas. Sounds so sexy," she laughed.

"We forget Texas. That's where they shoot the President. I used to want to see Texas."

"Why the hell would you want to go someplace where they would shoot a president?"

"I used to want to go to Texas because of that film. You remember *The Yellow Rose of Texas*?"

Diane, laughter on every word, began to sing "The Yellow Rose of Texas, Was the only girl for me… e… e… e."

"Yeah, I know. Go ahead and laugh at me," Velma hung her head in mock shame. "It wasn't real, okay? Just like all those other things we believed."

She came back to the table. "They shooting ordinary people up here too, not just presidents. You see in the papers how the police in New Jersey kill some black people? We have to be careful, Dee. In Trinidad, we didn't have to be frightened to walk the streets because we have black skin, Up here, we could get killed for that." She sighed deeply. "When? When you think we'll ever be able to see some place other than this nasty New York? We working day and night."

Diane reached for her letter and began to fold it in three so that the two fifty-dollar notes she would insert would not fall out. "I'm not going to spend all my time in this country working in no hospital kitchen. As soon as I get my business fixed, I'm applying for a better job somewhere else so I could put aside the money to go to university. I would never have that chance in Trinidad. One thing America gives you is a chance, girl, hard-arse place as it is, and I intend to take it."

"Me too," Velma admitted. "But is a lot we have to contend with that we never had to suffer at home. Here, when people see us, the first thing come to their mind is skin colour. You can see it in their eyes. It wasn't like that back home. And then this blasted winter. It's only October, and I'm freezing."

"When Spring comes, we won't even remember feeling the cold," Diane said. "That's something to look forward to."

"Okay, then." Velma picked up her pen and held it poised over her letter. "You describe spring for me, and I'll write about it. That will be better than pretending America is paved with fifty-dollar bills."

"Don't get so serious, girl," Diane laughed. "What's the point in worrying them back home, eh? What they could do about anything here? Besides, what we going through up here is nothing compared to what they have to contend with."

"I'm waiting to hear your description of spring," Velma said. "You see any daffodils? Maybe I'll draw a few daffodils on the page like the ones we used to read about in the English poetry books."

Diane shook her head. "What daffodils? I see any daffodils?"

"Okay then," Velma persisted. "How about lilacs? Remember that poem Mr. Carimbocas made us learn? It was by an American poet, Walt something."

"Walt Whitman," Diane said softly. "'When Lilacs Last in the Dooryard Bloom'd!' I remember it because I like the word 'dooryard'."

"And because you got licks on your knuckles when you skipped a verse." Velma laughed. "Don't think I forget that."

"That was a long damn poem." Diane grinned at the memory of herself standing up in front of the school on Speech Day, and embarrassing herself, her parents, and most of all, Mr. Carimbocas. " 'When lilacs last in the dooryard bloom'd'," she recited, "'and the great star early droop'd in the western night, I mourn'd, and yet shall mourn with ever-returning spring.' That was a damn sad poem. But it didn't seem so at the time."

"So they looked the way he described them? They have 'heart-shaped leaves of rich green/With many a pointed blossom rising delicate, with the perfume strong'?" Velma recited.

Diane shook her head, "Couldn't say. I don't remember seeing a single flower last spring. Not a lilac, not a daffodil, not even a damn rose. Umm umm um."

"But you were here," Velma insisted. "You were here in spring."

Diane nodded. "Yeah. But when I leave this house foreday morning, I don't come back till midnight. You're forgetting I have two jobs? And on Saturday it's clean, clean, clean this place. On Sunday, I do the laundry, study my books. When I have time to see spring? Stupes."

"So," Velma pushed away her letter again. "We have to lie about spring, too. You don't even know for sure if Walt Whitman was writing the truth 'bout lilacs."

"Just like you believe *The Yellow Rose of Texas*, right?" Diane said softly. "If we have to lie, maybe those writers lied too."

"Okay then," Velma said with false cheerfulness. "Let's be writers. Let's tell some lies. I'll draw some flowers that look like daffodils and lilacs. Ma and Tante Lill wouldn't know the difference anyway." In the margins of the lined page she scribbled botanical designs. Diane looked away.

At the bottom of her letter, Velma stopped drawing to write:

> *I know you have to have new curtains for Christmas, Ma, so next month I will send $50 for you to buy some cloth. But don't give it to Miss Irma to make. She sews too puckity. Put the $50 I'm sending you now as a down payment on a stove in the Syrian man's store. I promise I will send the rest next paycheck to pay it off so you'll have it in time to cook on for Christmas. Don't worry. Everything is fine with me. Diane sends her regards. She's doing very well. Tell Camille and Jenna I will send them a big box of clothes and shoes for Christmas.*
>
> *Your loving daughter,*
> *Velma*

As if she had read the letter, Diane said, "So you still not telling them what that man do to you? Eh? He made you lose your job with Nina Simone. Your belly's big and God knows if you'll be able to keep working in the hospital after the baby comes, but you still promising to send down all kind of things. So who telling stories now, eh? Tell me that. Who's lying?"

Velma could not look at Diane as she said, "I just have to hope and pray everything will turn out okay. Is America, right?"

Diane sealed up her envelope without responding.

In front of the crystal vase on the sideboard in the dining room, the girls placed their letters for Mrs. Charles to find. Since they left for work early, and did not return before the post office closed, she would register the letters for them with return receipt requested. Diane had heard stories from friends at the hospital about people at home stealing letters coming from America.

As they were unfolding Mrs. Charles's tablecloth to lay it

neatly back on the table, Diane said to Velma, "You hear that man on the radio last night? He was talking about all the stresses and strife black people undergo in America. I like what he say at the end. 'Ain't no monkey goin' stop this show, Baby'. We need to remember that. Ain't no monkey goin stop this show."

Velma laughed as she repeated the line with Diane who was doing a jig around the table.

The two Alabama girls with whom they shared the upstairs of Mrs. Charles's house paused on their way out the door to shake their heads in wonder. Those West Indian girls were so happy, they were always finding something to sing and dance about.

TO DIE OF OLD AGE IN A FOREIGN COUNTRY

They think I can't remember things because I'm getting old and I can't see so good. I have two cataracts. But I am eighty-four years old this September. A Virgo. And I does read my horoscope book every day as God send. They think I going down. Huh. What they know? I live my four score already and I'm still here. I'm luckier than most. Look how Miss Ivy dead. And Valto too. He thought he would outlive me but God outsmart him. I am still going strong. And I'm not forgetting ONE damn thing.

My birthday is sixth of September 1906. I live a long time, oui. You don't think so? I am the last of my brothers and sisters. My mother make twelve of us. Poor Vivian, my last sister, died five years ago this month. Twenty-fifth of March 1985. I was over here, but you know what? They didn't tell me she died until they had put my one last sister in the ground and throw dirt on top of her. You could imagine that? My one last sister. She was two years older than me. We grow up together. Jenna and the rest of them say I wouldn't be able to take the news. I might have dropped down. You could imagine that? I was so damn vexed with them for keeping that news from me. My one last sister. These young people always think they know best what to do for old people, but I still have a lot of crosses to bear. I could handle death.

If I was home, I would have washed my sister myself and put white powder on her face, and sing Amazing Grace before they put her in the hole. But I'm in this foreign country getting old day by day, and all my life passing me by. Vivian had two thick-thick gold bracelets. You can't get gold like that these days. Jenna take them. That's why she didn't want me to come home for the funeral. She wanted to take my sister's gold bracelets. But I tell you, one day one day congotay. Those gold bracelets was to go to me. My Tantie

Mille gave them to Vivian in 1913, and she told Vivian to pass them on to me. But that thiefing Jenna, she's my daughter back home, she take them. Corbeaux will pick out her eyes for that.

God forgive me, I shouldn't curse my daughter. Jenna is a Godsend. She had a bad, bad husband. He give her a lot of children, seven boys and nine girls and I remember all their birthdays. You know how many grandchildren I have? Seventy-eight. Count them. Seventy-eight grandchildren. Fifty of them is girls. And I have forty-nine great grand. All Jenna's daughters have children. And bad, bad husbands. Poor she. She has her hands full day in and day out since Leroy dead. I'm glad she keep the gold bracelets. Tantie Mille get those gold bracelets from down the Main when Agard come back from working in the oilfields on July seventh, 1913. You can't get gold like that these days. Better Jenna have them to pawn. She has sixteen children in the house to feed, ten of them my great grand.

All those children breaking down my poor little house. Is my house they're living in, you know, because they lost theirs years ago. I remember the day. Ninth of June 1962. Leroy gamble the house away. Jenna cried once and she never cry again. She's strong like me. And she is quiet, God rest the dead. She is Mother Theresa. Everybody comes to her and say, "Miss Jenna, I can't take care of my child. You could help me?" Jenna taking the child. My poor house is an orphanage. Valto and I pour the first cement for the foundation on May eleventh, 1943. I'm not going to have any house to live in when I go back home. I want to go back home, you know. I don't want to die in this country. It's too cold. But what house I will have, eh? Tell me that. Jenna's taking every-body's children, and the people don't give her a cent to mind them. But somehow she does manage. She should have been a nun. She has pictures of the Pope stick up all over my house like wallpaper and I'm Nazarene. She's high up in the church, you know. They're always calling on her to go and tend to somebody sick. And she herself have so much troubles, oui.

She had troubles with Leroy when he was alive, and she had troubles when he died. On the day she was burying him, some Indian woman come to the burial ground making a big commess for them to pass her child over Leroy's grave. The woman say the child belong to Leroy. You could tell me what a young young girl like that was doing with a grown man who had nine children with his wife? Young people too worthless these days, oui. She come making big bacchanal in the cemetery. But look my crosses, nuh. If I was there, I would have hit that woman one slap in her face! But I was up here. It's a sad sad thing to be living in this foreign country when your family die at home. My whole life passing me by.

All my sons dying out.

Kenneth died last year. Heart attack. He just drop down. He was my oldest son. It's bad luck for a mother to see her son dead, old people say.

Right after that, Noel die. He was my third son. Laundryman. Cancer. He had nice gold teeth in the front. He died in Tobago. Gary never come back from his sea bath.

And then my darling son, Nate. He was my fourth son. .I name him after my brother in Tobago. I make seven boys, you know. Is seven or eight? And seven girl children too. Four of them die before they could get christened. They tell me it was bad luck for me to go, but I went to bury him. And I overhear them shoo-shooing that he died from AIDS.

I ask them why. Why they didn't tell me? They say they didn't think I could take it. I couldn't take it? ME? I who take so much already? I who bring all those children into this world? I who live to see so much beyond my time and more. My back is a cement block.

I went and kissed my son. They tried to hold me back, but I went and kissed my son. And I brush his hair back from his forehead, and I pat his face with white powder, and I sing Amazing Grace, how great though art, to have given me a son like this. They tried to hold me back; to keep me from kissing my own son, but I didn't let them.

I want to go home. I stay too long up here. Since August seventeenth, 1973. That's when I first come. Too long now. I tell Jenna, send for me. I don't want to end my days in this foreign country with all my life passing me by. I tell her to pick out a spot just where they plant the bamboo, near my sons, so when I stretch out my arms, I could hold them.

I hope she remember.

135

SMALL MERCIES
(*A Woman's Calypso*)

We get cuss too bad.
They say we work obeah
voodoo, pocomania
we turn soucouyant
give men things
to make them stupid.
We drink bush tea
to throw way baby.
They call we batty mamselle
whore names like Jean and Dinah
Mathilda and Clementina.
They say we saltfish stink
we don't trim we armpits.
They cuss we mother
throw firewater on we back
and chop we up with cutlass.
From dry season to when rain fall,
we live pressure.
Government don't help
Church can't do nothing at all.
We life in we own hands
all we could do is ban we belly and bawl.
What could we do?
We say praise God we have some food to eat
and the children not walking barefoot in the street
because in this life from morning to night
we holding strain, we waiting, not liming,
just waiting.

ABOUT THE AUTHOR

Brenda Flanagan was born in Trinidad in 1949. She started writing poetry at the age of ten and by thirteen she was singing calypsos and earning money for it. Later, she worked for a time in a factory, then was taken on as a trainee reporter of *The Nation*, the newspaper of the then ruling People's National Movement led by Dr. Eric Williams.

In 1967 she left Trinidad for the USA, working initially as a domestic servant. Marriage and motherhood deflected her plans to study, but by 1975, then a single mother, she began undergraduate studies at the University of Michigan. There she won prestigious Hopwood Awards for her short stories, a novel and drama.

She is the author the prizewinning novel, *You Alone Are Dancing* (Peepal Tree Press) and its sequel, *Allah in the Islands* (2009).

Brenda Flanagan teaches creative writing, Caribbean and African American Literatures at Davidson College, North Carolina. She is also a United States cultural ambassador, and has served in Kazakstan, Chad and Panama.

You Alone Are Dancing
ISBN: 9780948833335; pp201; pub. 1990; price: £7.99

Threatened by land speculators and ignored by a corrupt and uncaring government, the people of Roseville begin a fight for survival. In the midst of this struggle, Sonny Allen and Beatrice Salandy, burdened by the community's expectations and their own ambitions, have to work out their commitments to each other. Set on the fictional island of Santabella, *You Alone are Dancing* is a lyrical ballad woven from the villager's collective voices, though when a grievous wrong is done to Beatrice, she discovers the harsh truth of the novel's title.

Two kinds of crime are contrasted in this novel: the crimes of the wealthy and powerful and those of the poor. The first, the theft of village land by land speculators and a rape, go unpunished, until Beatrice takes the law into her own hands.

Brenda Flanagan's novel takes place in a calypso world of bobol and tricksterish deceptions and when the villagers of Roseville can take no more and pelt the visiting PM, Melda makes up an instant calypso to celebrate the occasion. It is a good one, not surprisingly when the author, by the age of thirteen, was singing calypsos and earning money for it.

"Every character lives and breathes... a captivating novel" – Roberta Mock, *Leeds Other Paper*.

Allah in the Islands
ISBN: 9781845231064; pp 216; pub. 2009; price: £8.99

The novel returns to the aftermath of the trial of Beatrice Salandy and to the villagers of Rosehill on the island of Santabella first met in Flanagan's novel *You Alone Are Dancing*. Though Beatrice is acquitted to the villager's joy, nothing much has changed. Though Santabella has been independent for several decades, only the new Black ruling class has benefited. Most Santabellans struggle to scratch a living, find adequate schools, healthcare or even reliable basic services. Cynical corruption flourishes and the queues to get visas to escape to America grow ever longer and more desperate.

But there is one new element: a rapidly growing radical Muslim movement with a growing appeal to the poor and Black with their welfare schemes, grass-roots campaigning and air of incorruptibility. And there is the Haji, the charismatic leader of movement who combines a media-savvy native wit, a well-developed mystique and a steely control over his group. Even Beatrice becomes, against her better judgement, drawn into Haji's orbit, though other more personal issues also demand decision.

"*Allah in the Islands* is more than a social commentary. It's a story about people and how they affect everything around them with the decisions they make in life. It's a story that makes you reflect on the roads we choose to take and the ones we pass by."

Los Angeles Sentinel